The Secret of Skeleton Island

This Armada book belongs to:

_____

_____

_____

Alfred Hitchcock and
The Three Investigators
in

The Secret of
Skeleton Island

Text by Robert Arthur

Armada

First published in the U.K. in 1968 by
William Collins Sons & Co. Ltd., London and Glasgow.
This edition was first published in Armada in 1970 by
Fontana Paperbacks,
14 St. James's Place, London SW1A 1PS.

This impression 1981

Printed in Great Britain by
Love & Malcomson Ltd., Brighton Road,
Redhill, Surrey.

WARNING! Proceed with Caution!

THE ABOVE WARNING is meant for you if you are of a nervous nature, inclined to bite your fingernails when meeting adventure, danger and suspense. However, if you relish such ingredients in a story, with a dash of mystery and detection thrown in for good measure, then keep right on going.

For this is the sixth adventure that I have introduced for The Three Investigators, and I can only say that never have they been in any tighter spots than they encounter here. You don't have to take my word for it—read the book and see!

Just in case you haven't met The Three Investigators before, they are Jupiter Jones, Pete Crenshaw, and Bob Andrews, all of whom live in the town of Rocky Beach, on the Pacific Ocean a few miles from Hollywood, California. Some time ago they formed the firm of The Three Investigators to solve any riddles, enigmas or mysteries that might come their way, and so far they have done well.

Jupiter Jones, the First Investigator, is the brains of the firm. Pete Crenshaw, the Second

Investigator, is tall and muscular and excels at athletics. Bob Andrews, the most studious of the three, is in charge of Records and Research.

Now on with the show! Turn the page and travel with the Three Investigators to Skeleton Island!

ALFRED HITCHCOCK

1

A Case for The Three Investigators

"How are you lads at Scuba diving?" Alfred Hitchcock asked.

Across the big desk from him in his office at World Studios, The Three Investigators—Jupiter Jones, Pete Crenshaw and Bob Andrews—looked interested. It was Pete who answered.

"We've just been checked out on our final tests, sir," he said. "Our instructor took us down to the bay day before yesterday and okayed us."

"We're not exactly experienced, but we know what to do and all the rules," Jupiter added. "And we have our own face masks and flippers. When we do any diving, we rent the tanks and breathing apparatus."

"Excellent!" Mr. Hitchcock said. "Then I think you are definitely the three lads for the job."

Job? Did he mean a job investigating some mystery? Mr. Hitchcock nodded when Bob asked him the question.

"Yes, indeed," he said, "and doing some acting, too."

"Acting?" Pete looked doubtful. "We're not

actors, sir. Although Jupiter did some acting on TV when he was a very small kid."

"Experienced actors aren't needed," Mr. Hitchcock assured them. "Natural boys are what they want. I'm sure you know, Pete, that your father is at the moment in the East working with director Roger Denton on a suspense picture called *Chase Me Faster*."

"Yes, sir." Pete's father was a highly experienced movie technician and his job took him all over the world. "He's in Philadelphia right now."

"Wrong." Mr. Hitchcock seemed pleased at Pete's astonishment. "Right now he's on an island in Atlantic Bay, down on the south-east coast of the United States, helping rebuild an old amusement park for the final scene of the picture. The name of the island is Skeleton Island."

"Skeleton Island! Wow!" This came from Bob. "It sounds like a pirate hangout."

"It was indeed once a pirate hangout," the director told them. "Skeleton Island—a strange and sinister name! A ghost is said to haunt it. Bones are still uncovered in its sands. Sometimes when the sea is stormy, a gold doubloon washes up on its beaches. However, before you get your hopes up, let me say there is no treasure on the island. That has been proved. There may still be small bits of treasure scattered on the bottom of the bay but none on Skeleton Island."

"And you want us to go there?" Jupiter Jones asked eagerly. "You say there's a mystery to be solved?"

"It's like this." Mr. Hitchcock put the tips of his fingers together. "Your father, Pete, and a couple of other men are camped there, using local workmen to fix up part of the park for the final scenes of the movie, most of which is being shot in Philadelphia.

"They're having trouble. Pieces of equipment have been stolen, and their boats have been tinkered with at night. They have hired a local man as a guard, but the nuisance hasn't stopped, just slowed down.

"Skeleton Island is picturesque and the waters of Atlantic Bay around it are shallow. Roger Denton thought that as long as he is working on the island, his assistant, Harry Norris, could direct a short subject about three boys on a holiday who dive for pirate treasure for fun."

"Yes, sir, an excellent idea," Jupiter said.

"It would cost very little more, and the company has a man, Jeff Morton, who is an expert diver and underwater photographer. That's where you come in. You boys could be the three actors, do enough Scuba diving to qualify, and on your time off wander round the town, hunting for clues to this mysterious thievery. We will keep your identity as investigators secret, so no one will suspect you."

9

"That sounds great!" Bob said with enthusiasm. "If our families will let us go."

"I'm sure they will, with Mr. Crenshaw there, too," Mr. Hitchcock said. "Of course, the mystery may not amount to anything, but in view of your past record, you may discover more than any of us suspect."

"When do we start?" Pete asked.

"As soon as I can make the arrangements with Mr. Denton and your father, Pete," Alfred Hitchcock said. "Go home and pack and be ready to fly East tomorrow. Here, Bob, since you are in charge of Records and Research, you may want to look at these articles about Skeleton Island—how it was discovered, the pirates who once made their headquarters there, and other interesting data. Familiarize yourself with it. The trip should be an interesting experience for you."

2

An Unexpected Meeting

"THERE'S Skeleton Island!" Bob Andrews exclaimed.

"Where? . . . Let me look!" Jupiter and Pete exclaimed. They leaned over Bob to peer out of the window of the sleek silver airliner.

The plane was gliding down over a long narrow bay—Atlantic Bay. Bob pointed to a small island almost directly below them. Its shape bore a curious resemblance to that of a skull.

"I recognize the shape from the maps Mr. Hitchcock gave us," Bob said.

They stared at the island with eager curiosity. Skeleton Island had once, more than three hundred years before, been a pirate hangout. Although Mr. Hitchcock had said there was no pirate gold buried there, maybe he was wrong. Maybe there was still some treasure to be found. They hoped so. In any case, the island held a mystery which they would attempt to solve.

Another island, much smaller, came into view.

"Then that must be The Hand!" Jupiter said.

"And those are The Bones," Pete added, pointing to a scatter of narrow reefs between Skeleton Island and The Hand. "Golly, think of it! We left Rocky Beach after lunch and here we are in time for dinner."

"Look," Bob said. "The Hand *does* look sort of like a hand. The fingers are rocky reefs that are under water most of the time, but from up here they're very clear."

"I hope we get a chance to explore The Hand," Jupiter said. "I've never seen an actual blowhole before. That magazine article Mr. Hitchcock gave us said that in a storm, water spouts out of the blowhole just like a whale."

Now the islands fell behind them. So did the small village on the mainland called Fishingport which was their immediate destination. A room was waiting for them there at a boarding house.

As the plane slid down out of the sky, a fair-sized city appeared on their right. This was Melville, where the airport was. A few moments later the boys were unfastening their seat belts as the plane rolled to a stop in front of the air terminal building.

They climbed down the stairs and stood looking around them at the small crowd which waited behind a wire fence.

"I wonder if your dad will meet us, Pete," Bob said.

"He said he'd try to, but he would send someone else if he couldn't," Pete answered. "I don't see him."

"Here comes someone who seems to be looking for us," Bob said in a low voice as a short, pudgy man with a red nose approached them.

"Hi," he said. "You must be the three kid detectives from Hollywood. I was told to pick you up." He stared at them with small, shrewd eyes. "You don't look much like detectives to me," he said. "I thought you'd be older."

Bob felt Jupiter stiffen. "We're supposed to act in a picture," he said. "Why do you think we're detectives?"

The man gave them a broad wink.

"There isn't much I don't know," he said with a grin. "Now follow me. I have a car waiting. There will be another car to pick up your baggage—got a lot of stuff coming in from Hollywood on this plane, too much for my car."

He turned and led them out of the gate to an old station wagon.

"Hop in, boys," he said. "It's a good half-hour's ride and by the looks of it, we're in for a storm."

Bob looked up at the sky. Although the sun still shone, low on the horizon, black clouds were whipping towards them from the west. A flicker of lightning played along the front of the clouds. It did look as if a storm was coming, a real whopper.

The boys climbed into the back seat, the man got in behind the wheel, and the station wagon started away from the airport, heading north.

"Excuse me, Mr. ——" Jupiter began.

"Just call me Sam," the man said. "Everybody calls me Sam."

As he spoke, he stepped on the gas and the car hurtled along at a high speed. The sun had gone behind a cloud, and suddenly it was almost dark.

"Excuse me, Mr. Sam," Jupiter asked, "but do you work for the movie company?"

"Not regularly, boy," Sam answered. "But I agreed to pick you up as a favour. Say, look at that storm coming. This will be a good night for the phantom of the merry-go-round to show

13

herself. I wouldn't want to be out on Skeleton Island tonight."

Bob felt little prickles of excitement go up his spine. The phantom of the merry-go-round! The magazine articles they had studied so carefully had told them all about the ghost that supposedly haunted Skeleton Island. According to legend, it was the ghost of lovely but headstrong Sally Farrington, a young woman who had been riding the old merry-go-round one night twenty-five years before.

A sudden storm had blown up and the merry-go-round had stopped. Everyone else had got off, but Sally Farrington refused to climb down from her wooden horse. According to the legend, she cried out that no storm was going to stop her from finishing her ride.

As the operator of the merry-go-round was arguing with her, a bolt of lightning had crackled down from the sky and struck the metal pole in the middle of the carousel. To the horror of everyone, Sally Farrington was killed.

Her last words had been, "I'm not afraid of any storm and I'm going to finish this ride if it's the last thing I ever do!"

Everyone agreed that the tragedy was her own fault. But no one was prepared for what followed. A few weeks later, one stormy night when Pleasure Park was closed down and empty, people on the mainland saw the lights of the merry-go-round blaze up. The wind brought

14

the sound of carousel music to their ears.

Mr. Wilbur, the owner of the park, had taken some men in a boat to investigate. They got close enough to the island to see the merry-go-round spinning and a white-clad figure clinging to one of the painted horses.

Then the lights had abruptly gone out and the music stopped. When the men reached the scene a few minutes later, they found the park utterly deserted. But lying on the ground beside the carousel they found a soaking wet handkerchief, tiny and feminine, with the initials "S.F." embroidered on it. It was easily recognized as one of Sally Farrington's handkerchiefs.

A wave of superstitious fear spread among the townspeople. It was said that Sally's ghost had come to finish her interrupted ride. The amusement park soon had a reputation for being haunted. Many people stayed away from it, and the following year it had not reopened. The roller coaster, the Ferris wheel, the merry-go-round—everything had been left to rot and decay as the years passed.

But the legend of Sally Farrington's ghost did not die. Fishermen claimed to have seen it, especially on stormy nights, wandering about the island. In the last few years it had been reported a dozen times, sometimes by two or more men. The popular belief was that Sally Farrington was doomed to haunt the island, waiting to finish her fatal ride on the merry-go-round. And now that the merry-go-round was no longer able to run, she would wait for ever.

Therefore Skeleton Island had been deserted for years. There was no real reason to go there, with the amusement park closed, except perhaps to have a picnic in the summer. And picnickers were few and far between because of the island's reputation.

"I hear," Sam called back to the three boys, "that these motion-picture fellows are fixing up the old merry-go-round again. Sally's ghost will be mighty happy about that. Maybe if it gets running again she can finish her ride."

He chuckled. Then, as the first wind from the approaching storm struck them, he devoted himself to driving.

They were driving through what seemed to be marshy, empty country. After half an hour, they came to a fork in the road. The main road turned left and in the headlights the boys could see a sign pointing in that direction: *Fishingport: 2 miles.* To their surprise, Sam turned the car down the unmarked road to the right, which soon became two sandy ruts.

"The sign said Fishingport was the other way," Pete spoke up. "Why are we going this way, Mr. Sam?"

"Necessary," Sam said over his shoulder. "Been a crisis. Mr. Crenshaw wants you to come straight out to the island instead of going to Mrs. Barton's in town tonight."

"Oh, I see." Pete subsided. They all wondered what the crisis was. Had something very serious happened?

After bumping along the sandy road for a couple of miles, the car stopped. The headlights showed a rickety pier. Tied to the pier was a small, rather dilapidated fishing boat. "Out you get, boys!" Sam cried. "Lively now! That storm's ready to bust loose."

They climbed out of the car, a little surprised that the movie company didn't have better transport than this. But probably it was Sam's own boat.

"Will our baggage follow us?" Jupiter asked as Sam joined them.

"Your baggage is safe and sound, boys," Sam said. "Climb in now. We've got a ride ahead of us."

They climbed into the boat. Sam bent over the motor. He turned a switch and the heavy flywheel began to spin. Soon they were chugging out into the choppy water, all three boys hanging on for dear life as the small craft pitched and plunged.

Then the rain came. First it was a fine pelting spray mingled with tiny hailstones. Next came the big drops. The boys, crouched under a thin canvas cover, were soon soaked.

"We need raincoats!" yelled Pete to Sam. "We'll be the first boys to drown above water in Atlantic Bay!"

17

Sam nodded and lashed the wheel. He went to a locker and pulled out four yellow plastic slickers with hoods. He put one on himself and handed the others to the boys.

"Get into these," he yelled. "I keep 'em for fishing parties."

Jupiter's was too tight to button and Bob's was much too long. But they kept out the rain.

Sam went back to steering. Now the sky was a bombardment of thunder. The tiny boat tipped dangerously in the high waves, and the boys were afraid that any moment they would overturn.

After what seemed a long time, they could see land ahead, lit by lightning flashes. They saw no dock or pier, and were surprised when Sam pulled the boat alongside a flat rock that projected out into the water.

"Jump ashore, boys!" he yelled. "Lively now!"

Puzzled, The Three Investigators leaped from the boat to the rock.

"Aren't you coming, Mr. Sam?" Jupiter called as the boat started drifting away.

"Can't," Sam yelled back. "Follow the trail to the camp. You'll be all right."

He gunned the motor. In a moment the boat had vanished into the stormy night.

The boys bent their heads against the pelting rain.

"We better try to find that path!" Pete shouted. Jupiter nodded.

Then Bob heard a strange sound, like a great beast breathing hoarsely.

"Whooooo-*whish!*" it went. "Whooo-*whish!*"

"What's that sound?" he shouted. "Listen!"

Again came the strange noise. "Whoo-*whish!* Whoo-*whish!*"

"Something on the island," Jupiter answered. "Let's see if we can see it when the next lightning comes."

They all stared inland. Then came a vivid bolt of lightning. By its brilliant light they could see they were on a rather small island, certainly not big enough to be Skeleton Island.

This one was all rocks, with a hump in the middle and a few straggly trees. There was no path, and no camp. And just before the sky darkened again, they saw a plume of water shoot upward from the centre of the hump. It went up like a spouting geyser, and as it did so they heard the "Whoo-*whish!*" sound again.

"A spout!" Jupiter called. "It must come from a blowhole in the rocks. We aren't on Skeleton Island at all. We're on The Hand."

They looked at each other in dismay.

For some unknown reason, Sam had marooned them on The Hand, at night in a storm. And they had no way to get off or call for help.

19

3

The Phantom is Seen

JUPITER, Bob and Pete crouched beneath an overhanging rock. It wasn't completely dry, but it provided some shelter from the wind and rain. During the last few minutes, they had scrambled over enough of the little island to convince them it had to be The Hand, and that there was no one else on it, and no boat.

They had taken a close look at the curious spout, which shot up from the middle of a flat place on the rocky hump. Jupiter, whose scientific curiosity never flagged under any circumstances, explained that there must be a crack in the rock that went deep under the island. The waves of the storm forced water into it, to be expelled up the blowhole.

However, they hadn't lingered to study the spout. They had to find shelter. After more stumbling around, they had found the rocky crevice that protected them now.

"Sam's marooned us!" Pete said indignantly, wiping rain from his face. "Why did he do it, that's what I want to know?"

"Maybe he made a mistake and thought this really was Skeleton Island," Bob suggested.

"No." Jupiter shook his head. "He brought us here on purpose. I confess I am baffled as to his reason. I am also baffled by the fact that he knew we were investigators. There's something queer going on."

"I'll buy a double helping of that," Pete grumbled. "I only hope we don't starve to death on this island before someone finds us!"

"We'll be found in the morning," Jupiter said. "Some fishing boat will spot us. We'll just have to stick it out tonight."

"But there aren't any fishing boats up at this end of Atlantic Bay," Bob put in anxiously. "Don't you remember those articles we read? Some tiny red parasite has got into the oysters in this part of the bay. All the fishing boats have moved down to Melville, at the south end, where the shellfish are still safe to eat. Fishingport is almost a ghost town because of the sickness of the oysters."

"Someone will spot us," Jupiter said. "There will be a search on for us when it is learned we have disappeared. And at least we have seen the spout actually working."

There didn't seem much more to be said. Fortunately it was not too cold on the island, and the storm seemed to be letting up. The only thing they could do was wait for morning. When they had decided that, they relaxed. Soon they found themselves dozing off.

Suddenly Pete awoke. It took him a few

seconds to remember where he was and what had happened. Then he saw that the storm had passed. The stars were out. And out on the water a hundred yards away a light was flashing.

Pete leaped up and started to yell. In a moment, Bob and Jupiter were awake and struggling sleepily to their feet.

The light turned in their direction, like a probing finger trying to find them. Pete ripped off his yellow raincoat and waved it madly.

"Here, here!" he shouted.

The light caught the billowing raincoat and held. Whoever was out there had seen them!

The powerful beam of light pointed upwards, illuminating the sail of a small boat. Then it flickered along the shore and picked out a little beach. It held on that spot, bobbing as the boat moved.

"He'll land there," Pete said. "He wants us to meet him there."

"Luckily there is some starlight now." Jupiter observed. "Even so, we'll practically have to feel our way."

"Look!" Bob exclaimed. "He's trying to help us."

The flashlight was now flicking over the ground between the boys and the shoreline, showing them the way in brief glimpses.

They made the best time they could. Even so, they each fell down and Pete skinned his knee. By the time they reached the beach, a small sailing-boat was drawn up in the sand, the sail down. A boy in a windbreaker jacket and trousers rolled up to the knees stood on the sandy shore.

He flashed his light briefly over their faces, then reversed it to shine it on himself. They saw a tanned, smiling face topped by dark curly hair. Merry black eyes glinted at them.

"Ahoy!" he said, in a voice with a foreign accent. "You are the three detectives, yes?"

It seemed that everyone knew who they were.

"We're The Three Investigators," Jupiter said. "We're certainly glad you found us."

"I think I know where to look for you," the boy said. He was almost as tall as Pete, but skinnier, though he had powerful chest and arm muscles. "I am Chris Markos. Christos Markos, in full, but call me Chris, okay?"

"Okay, Chris," Pete said. They took an immediate liking to this smiling, cheerful boy who had come to their rescue. "How'd you know where to look for us?"

"Long story," Chris told them. "Climb in my boat, and we will sail to town. Movie people are very upset. We will make them feel better to see you."

"Aren't you part of the *Chase Me Faster* company?" Bob asked as they clambered into the tiny boat.

"No, not me," Chris said, shoving the boat off and wading after it. He climbed in the rear and

23

settled himself by the tiller. Soon the little sail had caught the breeze, and the boat began to cut through the water. In the distance the boys could see the lights of the little town of Fishingport.

Once the boat was under way, Chris Markos told them about himself. He had grown up in Greece, on the shores of the Mediterranean, where he had lived with his father, a sponge fisherman. His mother was dead. Greek sponge fishers went down great depths to gather sponges from the ocean bottom, using no diving apparatus except a heavy stone to take them down swiftly.

Chris's father, one of the most daring divers, had one day been afflicted by an attack of the bends, the dread of every diver. As a result he was partially disabled and had been unable to continue diving. But a cousin who was an oyster fisherman in Fishingport had sent money for him and Chris to come to the United States.

"For a few years, fishing goes well," Chris said. "Then oysters get sick. Little red bug gets into them. Oyster fishing around here is all finished. My father's cousin, he has to sell his boat. He goes to New York to work in a restaurant. But my father is not well enough. He gets worse from worrying. Now he is in bed almost all the time. I try to take care of him, but I have trouble getting a job. I hear movie company is coming to town, they maybe need a diver. I am a good diver. When I was a little boy,

I start practising to be a sponge fisher like my father. But movie people, they say no. They do not like me. Everybody is suspicious because I am a foreigner. Oh well, maybe luck will turn soon."

They were sailing along briskly now. The boys could hear the mutter of breaking waves, and see splashes of whitecaps off to their left.

"Where are we now?" Pete asked. "How can you find your way when you can't see what's ahead? You may crash on one of those rocks."

"I tell by the ears," Chris said cheerfully. "I hear waves break, and know reefs are off there. They are what some people call The Bones. Skeleton Island is off ahead, to the left."

The boys all peered ahead, trying to see Skeleton Island. They knew its history by heart, from studying the papers Alfred Hitchcock had given them.

Skeleton Island had been discovered in 1565 by an English sea captain, Captain White. He had explored the island briefly, discovering that it was used as a sacred burying ground by Indian tribes on the mainland. As the Indians did not bother about digging very deep graves, many skeletons had been found. Because of this, and its skeleton-like shape, Captain White had named it Skeleton Island. At the same time he had visited The Hand, noticed the reefs which made it seem like a hand, and so given it its name. Then he had sailed away.

In the years that followed, pirates had infested the whole south-eastern sea coast. They had used the island for winter quarters, and come to the mainland to spend their gold. Blackbeard himself had spent one winter there.

But gradually the British authorities began to crack down on the pirates. By 1717, after Blackbeard was dead, the only buccaneer left in the region was the notorious Captain One-Ear. One night the British troops had made a surprise attack on his quarters on Skeleton Island.

While his crew was being slaughtered, the captain himself had escaped with his treasure chests in a longboat. The British commander, as anxious to recover the gold as to exterminate the pirates, gave chase.

Captain One-Ear, finding he could not escape, made a final stand on The Hand. Here his remaining men were killed and he was captured, badly wounded. But the chests that the British had been so anxious to recover turned out to be empty. The treasure had disappeared. The Hand was too rocky for him to have buried the gold there, and the British could find no other hiding place. To all questions, Captain One-Ear gave only one laughing answer:

"Davy Jones has my gold doubloons in his grasp now, and he'll hold them tight until he decides to give them back. And that won't be until the crack o' doom!"

Even when he was hanged, he would say no

more, and the British commander was cheated of his spoils. It was obvious Captain One-Ear had dumped the treasure overboard, just to disappoint his pursuers. It was scattered over the sea bottom now, and no one could ever find it again.

The boys peered through the darkness, hoping to see the outline of the fabled Skeleton Island. It was too dark, however, to see anything.

"You must sail these waters a lot," Jupiter said to Chris, "if you can tell where you are by sound."

"Sure thing!" Chris agreed. "I sail all round here. Sometimes I dive, too. I look for gold— you know gold scattered over the bottom of bay."

"Yes, we know," Bob said. "Over the years quite a few doubloons have been found that way. Probably from the treasure Captain One-Ear dumped overboard."

"Have you found anything?" Pete asked.

Chris hesitated. Then he said, "Yes, I find something. Not a big something. But something."

"How did you find it, Chris?" asked Jupiter.

"I find it just last week," Chris said. "Only a little something, but who knows, maybe I will find more. Can't tell you where, though. Secret one person knows is a secret. Secret two persons know is no secret, Secret three persons know is knowledge shouted to the world. That is an old saying. Duck your heads, we come about on a new tack."

They ducked. The sail swung from one side to the other. The boat heeled the opposite way and started on its new tack, straight towards the lights of Fishingport.

"Skeleton Island is right behind us now," Chris said. "But we head for town."

Again the boys peered through the darkness, trying to see the island. Then Bob gasped.

"Look!" he yelled. "Lights!"

Suddenly in the darkness lights had appeared. They made a circular pattern, like the lights on a merry-go-round. Music — carousel music! — floated over the water. The lights started to revolve, slowly, then faster and faster. A moment later, a pale figure appeared, moving among the merry-go-round's painted horses.

"The phantom of the merry-go-round!" Pete cried. "It has to be—it's a girl in a white dress!"

"Chris, turn round!" Jupiter begged. "We have to investigate this."

"Not me!" Chris exclaimed. "That is the ghost all right. She is back to take her ride on the merry-go-round now the movie people have it fixed. We get away from here. Wish I had a motor, so we go faster!"

He kept the boat headed straight for Fishingport. Bob and Pete were rather glad, but Jupe was obviously disappointed. He itched to see a real phantom at close range.

28

Behind them the merry-go-round kept spinning, a blaze of lights in the darkness. Sally Farrington trying to finish her last ride, twenty-five years after she had died! Bob shivered at the thought.

Then, unexpectedly, the music stopped. The lights went out. The carousel and the white figure were gone. For some reason poor Sally Farrington had been unable to finish her last ride.

Jupiter sighed in disappointment. Half an hour later they were safe at Mrs. Barton's boarding house in Fishingport, and Mrs. Barton was spreading the news by telephone of their being found. She made Pete, Bob and Jupe take hot baths and get straight into bed.

They were glad to do so. But, just before he dozed off, Jupe murmured out loud, "I wish I could have got closer to the phantom!"

"That remark," replied Pete sleepily, "does not reflect the sentiments of the rest of The Three Investigators!"

Faster and faster went the merry-go-round.

4

Skeleton Island at Last

As BOB AWOKE, he was puzzled to see a slanting ceiling with striped wallpaper over his head. Then he remembered. He wasn't at home. He was three thousand miles from Rocky Beach, in a town called Fishingport, on Atlantic Bay.

He sat up and looked round. He was in the upper half of a double bunk. Below him Pete was fast asleep. In a bed a few feet away Jupiter Jones was also sleeping.

Bob lay back again, thinking over the strange events of the previous night.

There was a rap on the door. "Boys!" It was Mrs. Barton, the plump, cheerful landlady. "Breakfast is waiting, and Mr. Crenshaw is downstairs. Be down in five minutes or we'll throw it out!"

"We'll be there!" Bob leaped down to the floor. Pete and Jupiter, awakened by the voices, were soon dressed, and they all hurried downstairs. In a bright yellow dining room, decorated with various nautical objects, breakfast was waiting. Two men sat at the table, conversing in low tones and drinking coffee.

Pete's father, a large, ruggedly built man, jumped up as the boys entered. "Pete!" he exclaimed, putting an arm round his son. He shook hands with Bob and Jupiter. "I certainly was glad last night to hear you'd been found and were safe. By then you were asleep, so I hurried back to Skeleton Island. We have to guard our supplies and equipment every minute these days. But we'll come to that later. Right now I want your story."

As The Three Investigators ate, they took turns telling what had happened the night before. The other man, who was introduced as Police Chief Nostigon, nodded and puffed on a stubby pipe as he listened. While the boys got to the part about the man named Sam, Mr. Crenshaw turned to the police chief.

"This fellow Sam?" he asked. "Can you place him?"

"Sounds like Sam Robinson to me," the chief said, a trifle grimly. "Know him well. Been in jail a few times. Do anything for money, and likes to play practical jokes. Wonder if he could have been trying some crazy joke last night? Expect I'll have to ask him a few questions."

"That was no practical joke!" Mr. Crenshaw exploded. "I want to ask that fellow some questions myself. One, how he knew the boys were coming. Two, how he knew they were amateur investigators. And three, why he marooned them on that island. Why, we might

32

not have found them until today or tomorrow if that boy Chris hadn't rescued them!"

"That's a fact," the chief agreed. "When we learned you lads had got off the plane and then vanished into thin air, we were looking on land for you. Stopped cars for miles around to ask questions."

"What I want to know," said Mr. Crenshaw, "is how this kid Chris was able to find you so easily. What's his story?"

The three boys were forced to confess they had forgotten to ask him. They had meant to— then they had seen the merry-go-round and the ghostly figure of a woman on it, and in the excitement the question had slipped their minds.

"You saw the ghost?" Mr. Crenshaw exclaimed. "But that's impossible. The phantom of the merry-go-round is just a local superstition!"

"Now hold on a minute," Chief Nostigon said. "Folks around here believe in that phantom pretty strongly. The last few years, more'n one fisherman has seen it on a stormy night out on Skeleton Island. Hardly a soul will go near that island now.

"What's more, the whole town is buzzing about the phantom riding the merry-go-round last night. Lots of folks heard the music, and a few got out spyglasses and could see a white figure just like these boys describe it. I'm not saying I believe in ghosts, but you can't get a

33

soul in these parts to believe poor Miss Sally Farrington's spirit wasn't trying to ride that merry-go-round last night."

Pete's father shook his head. "This whole part of the picture is jinxed! I'll bet not a single workman shows up today."

"And maybe not tomorrow either," agreed Chief Nostigon. "Well, Mr. Crenshaw, I'll pick up Sam Robinson and ask him some questions. But we still don't know just how the boy Chris found these lads last night."

"It's darned suspicious, if you ask me," Mr. Crenshaw said. "That kid has been pestering me for a job, but he's got a bad reputation locally. Plenty of people say he's a clever little thief. I wouldn't be surprised if he had a hand in all the trouble we've been having."

"Chris didn't seem like a thief to us, Dad," Pete put in. "He seemed like an all-right kid. He has a sick father to help, and he sails round looking for washed-up treasure, but that's nothing against him."

"The boy's right," Chief Nostigon agreed. "I know Chris has a bad reputation, but he's a foreigner and most folks in this town are pretty clannish. They're ready to believe anything bad of a foreigner."

"Just the same, I have my suspicions of him," Mr. Crenshaw declared. "Now that I think of it, it could easily be a boy stealing our equipment. Maybe he's hoping to sell it to help his father."

He stood up. "All right, boys, let's get going. Mr. Denton himself is waiting out on the island for us. Chief, I'll be seeing you later. Meanwhile, I hope you can find this Sam Robinson and clap him in jail."

A few minutes later, Jupiter, Pete and Bob were in a fast motor-boat speeding to Skeleton Island. They would have liked to look round Fishingport more, but they didn't have time. They saw many docks and piers, but few boats—they understood that most fishermen had gone to the south end of Atlantic Bay where oystering was still safe and legal. All in all, Fishingport looked like a small and very poor fishing village.

Now, as the speedboat raced through the water, they eyed the island ahead with interest. It was a mile long, well wooded, and had a small hill towards the north end. They could barely see the remains of Pleasure Park through the trees. Across this mile of water, boats had once ferried gay crowds of merrymakers, but that day was far in the past.

They coasted in to an old pier at the south end of Skeleton Island, and Pete made a line fast. Another motor-boat was tied up there, a wide craft with special steps over the side—the kind of boat often used for Scuba diving.

Mr. Crenshaw led the boys up a well-marked trail. They soon reached a clearing where two trailers and several large, army-style tents had been set up.

"There's Mr. Denton," Pete's father said. "He drove down from Philadelphia yesterday for a conference and is going right back."

A young man wearing horn-rim glasses came towards them. Behind him three other men waited, one with greying hair who the boys soon learned was Harry Norris, the assistant director; a blond young man with a crew cut, who was Jeff Morton; and a big, barrel-chested man with a stiff left arm and a gun strapped to his waist who was Tom Farraday, the guard.

"This is our camp for now," Mr. Crenshaw went on. "We ferried the trailers and equipment over on a barge. The tents are all right until the main company gets here, then we'll need more trailers."

He pointed out and identified the other men, then spoke to Roger Denton, the director.

"Sorry to be a little late, Mr. Denton," he said. "I stopped to get the boys."

"Good," Roger Denton said. He looked rather upset. "Harry Norris has just been telling me about all the delays and I'm not happy about them. If you find you can't get the roller coaster working in a week, we'll forget Skeleton Island altogether. It's a great place for the scenery we want, but we may be able to save money by renting a roller coaster back in California and artificially ageing it. We can take back groundshots here that will give us the wonderful old, dilapidated effect."

36

"I'm positive we can get the roller coaster fixed," Mr. Crenshaw said. "I've got a call out for carpenters now."

"I doubt if you'll get them," Roger Denton said grimly. "Not since the whole town knows the ghost was seen riding the merry-go-round last night."

"That ghost!" Pete's father exclaimed. "I wish I could figure that out."

Tom Farraday, standing a few feet away, coughed apologetically.

"I'm very sorry, Mr. Crenshaw," he said. "I guess—well, I'm afraid I was the ghost folks saw last night."

5

The Skull Talks

"IT'S LIKE THIS," the guard explained as everyone stared at him. "Last night, I was here alone on guard when you all went to the mainland to look for the boys. When the storm hit, I took cover in a trailer. After the storm I heard a motor-boat, and I went out to see if maybe some thief had landed. I thought I saw a dark figure lurking behind the merry-go-round. As I started that way, I saw someone run away.

37

"I was worried that he'd been fooling with the motor, right after you got it fixed. So I turned on the lights and started it up. Of course the music started playing and the merry-go-round started turning. I walked round it, making sure there was no damage, then I turned it off."

"But the ghost, man, the ghost!" Mr. Crenshaw exclaimed.

"Well, sir—" Tom Farraday seemed embarrassed—"I was wearing a yellow storm slicker. And from a distance me in a yellow slicker probably looked enough like somebody in a white dress so that folks thought—well, you know."

"Oh, no!" Pete's father groaned. "Tom, you've got to go ashore later and tell everybody exactly what happened."

"Yes, sir," the guard said.

"As if we didn't have enough troubles already," sighed Mr. Crenshaw. "Well, we'll hire two more guards. Tom, look for two good men. None of these no-good fishermen who'll pretend to guard our equipment and then steal it—get honest men."

"Yes, sir."

"The idea of these boys doing a little private sleuthing for us on the quiet is no good now," Mr. Crenshaw said to Roger Denton. "Everybody in town seems to know they're boy detectives. That fellow Sam Robinson for one, though I'm blamed if I can figure out how."

"I think I can explain that, too, sir," Tom Farraday spoke up. "You see, when you and Mr. Denton were discussing the whole idea on the telephone with Mr. Hitchcock in Hollywood —well, most phones in this town are still on party lines. Other people can listen in. You know how it is in small towns. People snoop. It was probably all over town as soon as you hung up."

Mr. Crenshaw groaned. "That's what we're up against!" he said. "I'll be happy to get back to Hollywood. This Skeleton Island idea is turning into a jinx."

"We can get some beautiful shots here," Roger Denton said, "if you can get the roller coaster fixed up. Well, I have to get back to the mainland and start for Philadelphia. Jeff, suppose you ferry me over."

"Sure thing, Mr. Denton," the younger man said, and they started for the pier.

Mr. Crenshaw turned to the boys.

"Why don't I show you round while Jeff is gone?" he said. "As soon as he gets back, he'll see how well you boys can dive."

"Great, Dad!" said Pete.

A short walk brought them to a tumbledown fence. They walked over it and were in the abandoned amusement park. Pleasure Park really did look decayed. Refreshment stands were half caved in. The rides were rusty and falling apart. The Ferris wheel had toppled over in a storm and lay in pieces on the ground. An ancient roller coaster still stood upright, but with some timbers of its foundation dangling loose.

But the boys were most interested in the huge, old merry-go-round. Even in daylight, it had a spooky look, its paint peeling and new wood showing where Mr. Crenshaw's men had repaired it.

Mr. Crenshaw told the boys how it was to be used in the movie. "The way the picture is going to end is this: It's about a man who is falsely accused of a crime and is trying to find the true criminal. That's where the title comes from— *Chase Me Faster*. Finally the criminal hides on Skeleton Island here. Some young people row out for a picnic. They try the old merry-go-round, while the criminal secretly watches them."

"Golly, that sounds pretty exciting," Pete said.

"Where does the roller coaster come into it, sir?" Jupiter asked.

"The hero tracks the criminal here and starts to close in on him. The criminal abducts two girls from the picnic party and forces them into a car of the roller coaster. As the police surround him, he threatens to throw the girls over the side. The hero manages to get into the same car and there is a terrific fight at the end, as the old roller coaster swoops up and down and around."

"Terrific!" Bob said. "And in this spooky old

park it'll be the most! I can hardly wait to see it."

"If we shoot it here," Mr. Crenshaw said gloomily. "Well, we'll see. You boys can look round. Come back in half an hour. Jeff Morton ought to be back from the mainland by then."

He started away, then paused.

"Whatever you do," he said, with a look half worried and half humorous, "please don't find any treasure! Repeat, don't find any treasure! This was once a pirate hangout, you know."

"Yes, sir," Bob answered. "We've read all about the pirates and the treasure and the capture of Captain One-Ear."

"People never seem to give up," Mr. Crenshaw shook his head. "This island must have been dug up by large expeditions at least twenty times since then. Luckily, during the last fifty years not a doubloon has been found, so the treasure fever has died out. But knowing you boys, nothing would surprise me—not even your finding treasure where there isn't any!"

"Will it be all right, sir, if we explore the cave?" Bob asked. He pointed to the one hill on the island. "The old maps show a cave up at the top of that hill. The stories say it was used by the pirates to hold prisoners for ransom, but no treasure was ever found there."

"Yes, you can explore the cave," Mr. Crenshaw agreed. "But be back in half an hour."

He turned and walked away. The boys stood

41

staring round them at the ruins of Pleasure Park.

"It sure is creepy here all right," Pete said. "But that roller coaster scene will be terrific. It's scary just to think about."

"Jupe, you haven't said much," Bob said. "What're you thinking about?"

The First Investigator was looking very thoughtful.

"Your dad, Pete, and the others," he said, "seem to think that some of the fishermen are responsible for the thefts that have been going on, either for mischief or to steal something valuable. But I don't think so."

"You don't? What do you think?" Pete asked.

"The sabotage of the boats and the thefts of equipment," Jupiter said, "seem designed to get the movie company so fed up with Skeleton Island they'll move away and shoot the end of the picture somewhere else. This island has been deserted for twenty-five years and it is my deduction that someone wants it to stay deserted, and is deliberately trying to annoy Mr. Denton into abandoning the project."

"Want the movie company to leave!" Pete said blankly. "Why would anybody care if they left or not?"

"That is the mystery," Jupiter acknowledged. "Now let's go and see the old cave."

Ten minutes trudging uphill through scraggly trees brought them to a cave near the top of the rocky hill. The entrance was small, and the interior dark. However, once they were inside, there was light enough to see that they were in a roomy cave that went back quite a distance, narrowing towards the rear.

The soil of the cave was loose. It looked as if it had been dug up many times. Jupiter picked up a little of the sandy dirt and nodded.

"Many people have dug here for treasure," he said. "I daresay every inch of this cave was examined several times in the past hundred years. However, no sensible pirate would ever hide his treasure here. He'd look for a place less noticeable."

"Yeah," Pete agreed. "Wish we'd brought our flashlights. I'd like to look around in the back there."

"You're not as much of an investigator as I thought, Pete," Jupiter said, grinning. "You either, Bob. Look at me."

They looked with surprise as Jupiter unclipped a flashlight that was hanging from his belt.

"Primary equipment for any investigator," Jupiter said loftily. "However, I'll admit I remembered the cave, too, and planned on looking into it if we got the chance. Otherwise I might not have thought of it either."

He beamed the light towards the low back part of the cave. Some flat rocks looked worn smooth, as if imprisoned men had once lain on them as very hard beds. Jupiter's flashlight flicked over other rocky crevices and ledges until, at a point about six feet above the ground, it stopped suddenly.

Something white rested there on the ledge of a rocky shelf. Something white and round. Bob gulped. It was a human skull.

It seemed to grin at them. And then, just as Bob was reminding himself that it was only a bony memento of the bad old pirate days of long ago, the skull spoke to them.

"Go 'way," it sighed, with a strong accent that sounded Spanish to Bob. "Let me 'ave my rest. No treasure is here. Only my tired old bones."

6

Gold Doubloons

BOB FOUND that his feet had automatically turned to take him out of the cave. In another moment he and Pete were racing each other for the outside, with Jupiter not far behind. Bob and Pete collided and sprawled headlong at the entrance.

Jupiter, however, had turned back. He picked up the flashlight he had dropped and shone it on the skull.

"Skulls can't talk," he informed the aged death's head, "because to talk you need a tongue and larynx. Therefore logic tells me you did not speak."

Bob and Pete, picking themselves up outside the cave, suddenly heard whoops of laughter. Puzzled and a little embarrassed, they went back inside.

Chris Markos, the boy of the night before, was climbing down from a niche in the ricky wall.

"Hi," he said, tossing the old skull behind him. "Remember me?"

"Of course we remember you," Jupiter said. "In fact, I had already deduced it was you because earlier I saw a sailing-boat ahead of us that looked like yours. Besides, the voice that spoke was too youthful to be anything but a boy's."

"I scare you, yes?" Chris grinned. "You think dead pirate is talking to you."

"You startled me," Jupiter corrected him. "You scared Pete and Bob, though."

Bob and Pete looked sheepish.

"You didn't scare *me*," Bob said. "You scared my legs. I didn't know they were going to run until they did."

"Me, too," Pete agreed. "When a skull starts talking, my legs want to be some place else."

"Good joke!" Chris still radiated merriment.

"I hope you will not be mad, though. It is just for fun."

"No, we're not mad. We've been wanting to talk to you. Let's go outside in the sun." Jupiter led the way outside and all four boys stretched out, their backs against a rock.

"How did you happen to be here?" Jupiter asked the Greek boy. "I mean in the cave and everything, waiting for us?"

"Easy," Chris said. "I am sailing, and I see boat take you to the pier. I sail round the island and pull up my boat on the beach. I slip through trees, and see you at the old merry-go-round. I hear you say you are going to explore the cave. I know a short-cut, so I get there first. Then I think of this good joke with an old skull I know is up on one of the rocks. I climb up and hide and wait for you."

That explained everything, but Bob wanted to know why Chris had hidden. Why hadn't he come out and said hello earlier?

"The guard," Chris said simply. "That Tom Farraday always chases me away. Everybody chases me away."

His cheerful grin was suddenly gone.

"I have a bad name in town," he said slowly. "People think I am a thief, because my father and I are poor. And different. From a foreign country. In town are some people who are not good. They steal things and say Chris the Greek does it. But I do not do it!"

46

They believed him. It was an old trick, they knew, to blame things on an outsider.

"We believe you're honest, Chris," Pete said. "One thing puzzles us, though. How did you find us so quickly last night?"

"Oh, that," Chris said, grinning again. "I do some work in a place called Bill's Tavern. I sweep, wash dishes, get two dollars a day. My father and me, we live on that. Mr. Bill is a nice man."

"Two dollars a day!" Bob exclaimed. "How can you live on that?"

"Live in an old, abandoned fishing shack, no rent," Chris explained soberly. "We eat beans and bread and I catch many fish. But father, he is sick. He needs good food. So all the extra time I have, I sail around the bay, hoping to find big treasure. But I am foolish, I guess. Some treasure lies on the bottom of the bay. But what chance has Chris Markos to find lots of it?"

"You have as much chance as anybody!" Pete said. "But you were going to tell us how you knew where to look for us."

"Oh, sure. Yesterday I am washing dishes. I hear men talking in the last booth of tavern. One says, 'Three kid detectives, huh? Well, I'll hand them a surprise. I'll hand them something they won't forget!' Then they all laugh."

Jupiter pinched his lip thoughtfully. "Tell me, Chris, when this man spoke the word 'hand' did he do it with special emphasis?" he asked.

47

"He means did he say 'hand' in some special way?" Bob interpreted as the Greek boy looked puzzled.

"Oh, yes he does!" Chris exclaimed. "Each time he says 'hand' he makes the voice deeper and louder. So when I hear three boys are missing, I think to myself, where could anyone hide three boys? Then I remember the funny way that man says 'hand'."

"And you deduced that he was referring to the island called The Hand!" Jupiter exclaimed.

"That is just what I think. So I sail out as soon as the storm is over. And I find you right there, on The Hand. Only—" and Chris's face clouded again—"now movie people think that I had something to do with it. Nobody believes good of me."

"We believe in you, Chris!" Bob said stoutly.

Chris smiled. "You believe in me, I show you something."

His hand went beneath his pullover and out came a little well-oiled leather sack. Chris loosened the draw string.

"Hold your hands out," he said. "Close your eyes. Do not look until I say."

They obeyed. Something warm and heavy was placed in each boy's palm. When they opened their eyes, each was holding an antique gold piece!

Bob examined the worn, but still shiny coin. "Sixteen fifteen!" he exclaimed.

"Spanish doubloons!" Jupiter said, his eyes shining. "Real pirate treasure!"

"Golly!" Pete said in awe. "Where'd you find them?"

"In the water, lying on sand. There is plenty of treasure in bay — Captain One-Ear, he dumped his whole treasure overboard a long time ago. But now it's all scattered, a little here, a little there. Very hard to find any. I dive and dive. One piece I find off the other end of Skeleton Island, near wreck of nice yacht. But I find two right together in one special little bay where I think maybe——"

At that moment a loud, angry voice interrupted them.

"Hey! You, Chris! What're you doing here?"

Startled, they looked up. Tom Farraday, the normally good-natured guard, was puffing up the path towards them, his face dark with anger.

"I told you if I caught you hanging round any more, I'd give you a whaling!" Tom Farraday cried. "Those are my orders and——"

He stopped. The boys turned and followed his gaze. But Chris Markos had disappeared behind a rock as silently as a shadow.

7

Danger Underwater

"WHAT DID that kid want?" Tom Farraday
demanded. "Why did he bring you boys up
here?"

"He didn't want anything special," Jupiter
told him. "And he didn't bring us up here. We
came up to look at the cave."

"Well, let me tell you, that Chris is no good!"
the guard said. "If nobody's actually caught him
stealing anything yet, it's because he's too smart.
Take my advice and stay away from him. Now
come along. Jeff Morton is back and wants to
do some diving with you."

As they started down the trail, Tom's manner
became more friendly.

"I suppose you were hoping to find some
treasure in that cave," he said. "Well, there isn't
any and never was. What's left is scattered over
the bottom of the bay. Once in a long while a
piece turns up on a beach, but people have got
tired of even hunting for it any more, it happens
so seldom."

He chuckled.

"When Davy Jones takes something, he doesn't often give it back. Did you know that he took a hundred thousand dollars in good American cash only ten years ago? Yes sir, he took it and kept it. And because of that hundred thousand dollars my left arm got crippled and I've been this way ever since, only able to do odd jobs."

He moved his stiff left arm to show what he meant. The boys clamoured for the story, and Tom willingly obliged.

"Well, boys," he said, "I used to be a guard on an armoured car for the Dollar Delivery Company. One of our jobs was to pick up cash from the local banks and take it to the big national bank in Melville.

"Never had any trouble and didn't expect any. You see, we never followed the same route twice or went to the banks at exactly the same time. Just the same, one day—"

What had happened was that one day, about ten years before, they had stopped to pick up money from the bank in Fishingport. Then they had parked the armoured car to eat lunch. Naturally it was tightly locked, and they sat where they could see it.

However, as Tom and the driver left the restaurant, two men wearing Hallowe'en masks had stepped out of an old sedan and shot the driver in the leg. Tom had lunged at the men, but they had smashed him over the head and

51

shoulder with the barrel of the gun, knocking him unconscious.

Then they had taken the keys of the armoured car from his pocket, and driven off. But Chief of Police Nostigon, then a patrolman, had heard the shot and came running in time to fire at the two as they climbed into the stolen truck. He hit one of the robbers in the arm.

The alarm went out promptly, of course, and all nearby roads were bottled up. At nightfall the armoured car, bloodstained and empty, was found in an abandoned boat-house some miles away. It became apparent that the thieves had made their escape by water.

During the night a Coast Guard patrol boat sighted an old motor-boat drifting helplessly in the bay. As they closed in on it, two men were seen to dump several bundles overboard. They sank immediately.

When the Coast Guard boarded the boat, they found two men, Bill and Jim Ballinger, ready to give up. Their engine had broken down, and one of them, Jim, had a bullet wound in his arm. But not a scrap of money from the hold-up was found, then or later.

"You see, boys," Tom Farraday said, "they just chucked it overboard. Same thing old One-Ear did hundreds of years ago when he saw the British were going to catch him. It went to the bottom, sank in the mud, and no one could find it. Being paper money, it rotted away mighty fast."

"Golly!" Pete said. "That was quite an experience, Mr. Farraday. Did the Ballingers go to jail?"

"Oh, sure," the guard replied. "With the bullet from Chief Nostigon's gun in Jim's arm, they never had a chance. They went up for twenty years, but it was reduced to ten for good behaviour. They just got out a couple of weeks ago. I'd certainly like to pay them back for crippling my left wing, boys," Tom said fervently. "Haven't been much use since then— just odd jobs for me. Well, here we are and there's Mr. Crenshaw."

Pete's father and Jeff Morton were on the pier, stowing some gear into the big motor-boat. Mr. Crenshaw straightened as the boys came up.

"Hi, boys," he said. "Jeff is ready to check you out on your skin-diving. He's an expert diver and we have the very latest equipment here. He'll explain everything."

With that, Mr. Crenshaw left them, and the three boys climbed into the broad, roomy motor-boat.

"Okay, fellows," Jeff said. "Tell me what diving you've done."

Pete described the lessons they had had at a local swimming pool at home. They had become very familiar with snorkelling, and had been checked out by their instructor in Scuba diving just before coming East.

"So far, so good," Jeff said with an encouraging grin. "Now let's *see* how much you know."

He started the motor and ran the boat well out into the bay. Near a small yellow buoy, he dropped anchor.

"There's a wreck underneath us," he said. "No, it's not a treasure ship. Any old Spanish ship would long ago have disintegrated in these waters. This is a small yacht that went down in a storm several years ago. It lies in twenty-five feet of water, which means we can dive down to it without worrying about decompression problems."

He inspected and approved their face masks and flippers. Then, from a well-stocked equipment locker, he got out tanks of air, hose connections, and weighted diving belts.

"This is the latest equipment, and as nearly foolproof as it can be," he said. "We won't use wet suits because the water here is nice and warm. Get into your trunks, Bob, you'll take the first test dive with me. Remember, we'll be using the buddy system at all times—always two divers together."

The boys got into their swimming trunks, and Bob carefully put on the equipment Jeff handed him. Last of all he buckled on the weighted belt that would come off if he had to make a fast ascent.

Jeff inspected him critically, nodded his approval, and got ready to go over the side. Bob followed, using the special steps.

In the water, Bob kicked his flippered feet and shot downwards. He liked swimming. Over the years he had done a lot of it to build up strength in the leg he had broken as a small boy. Now, able to go down like a fish and breathe without difficulty, he felt wonderfully light and free, part of a new universe.

Below him a dark shape loomed up. It was the sunken yacht, and with Jeff at his side he swam slowly towards it.

The yacht lay on its side, a gaping hole near the bow. As they got closer, Bob could see that it was covered with seaweed. Small fish swam around it in swarms.

Jeff swam ahead. Using only his flippers to propel him, as he had been taught, Bob followed. Jeff swooped gracefully over the stern of the sunken yacht.

As Bob started to follow, his attention was caught by two large lobsters retreating beneath the stern. He swam closer to the sunken vessel.

Suddenly he was jerked to a stop.

Something had him firmly by his right ankle!

8

"Don't Tell Anyone!"

IT WAS the first time Bob had run into any
trouble underwater. A pang of alarm shot
through him and he kicked his leg to free it. The
grip on his ankle tightened. He was sure he
could feel himself being pulled backwards.

He turned frantically to see what had grabbed
him, and as he did so, his arm brushed his face
mask. The next thing he knew he was blinded.
Water had fogged the mask and for a second he
couldn't remember how to clear it.

Then something gripped his shoulder. For a
moment he was sure the monster, whatever it
was, was attacking him. But three light raps on
his air tank told him Jeff Morton had come back
to his rescue.

Jeff's hand gripped his shoulder, calming him.
Gradually Bob relaxed, though it did not release
him.

Forcing himself to breathe calmly, he turned
his head to the right, reached up, and cracked
the left side of his mask ever so slightly. Then he
breathed out through his nose. The air was

forced out of the mask, taking the water with it, and he could see again.

The first thing he saw was Jeff Morton, shaking his head. He pointed, and Bob looked down to see what had caught him. A loop of rope!

He doubled over and eased the rope off his flippered foot. Angry at himself for panicking, he shot ahead a few feet and waited for Jeff, expecting him to end the dive immediately. However, Jeff formed a circle with his thumb and forefinger, a sign everything was okay. Then he swam ahead again and Bob followed, carefully keeping clear of the wrecked ship.

They swam the length of the ship, then all round it, the fish moving aside for them as if they were just two harmless larger fish.

Bob saw more lobsters sheltering themselves under the yacht. If he had brought a spear gun, he was sure he could have bagged a lobster or two.

They swam until Bob was relaxed again and enjoying himself, then Jeff headed for the surface at an unhurried pace. They could see the bottom of the anchored motor-boat. A moment later they came up beside it, their masked faces popping from the water like the snouts of some strange monsters.

Jeff swam to the steps at the side of the boat and climbed it. Bob followed.

"How was it?" Pete said eagerly, helping him in the boat. Bob shook his head.

"I didn't do so well," he said. "I got snagged on a rope, and got panicky."

Jeff Morton agreed that he hadn't done so well. He gave them all a brief lecture on getting too close to tangled wreckage, and followed it with one on losing your head in an unexpected situation—the most dangerous thing a diver could do. Then he relented and smiled.

"Maybe it was a good thing it happened now," he said. "A harmless but helpful lesson. Bob recovered himself well and next time I'm sure he'll keep calm. All right, Pete, now it's your turn."

Pete got ready swiftly. In a moment the two divers were gone beneath the water, leaving Bob and Jupiter alone in the gently bobbing motorboat.

Bob told Jupiter of his experience in more detail, adding, "I think next time I go down I'll have more confidence. Now I know I can make myself act calm and clear my face mask if I have to."

Jupiter was about to reply when they heard a voice hailing them. A hundred yards away, the tiny sailing-boat owned by Chris Markos was gliding silently towards them.

Chris came up beside them and swung round, letting his sail flutter down. His white teeth

Fearfully he glanced behind him.

gleamed against his tanned face as he grinned at them.

"That fellow Tom Farraday tells you bad things about me, I guess," he said, his smile vanishing. "I hope you don't believe him."

"No," Bob said stoutly, "we don't believe him. We think you're all right, Chris."

"I am glad to hear that," Chris declared. He reached out and caught the side of the motor-boat to steady his craft.

He looked at the variety of diving gear in the motor-boat with some longing, but said airily, "Why do you need all that stuff to dive down to sunken yacht? I can go down that far just in my own skin. I'm a real skin-diver!"

"Is it true that Greek sponge fishers can go down more than a hundred feet without any diving apparatus?" Bob asked.

"Sure, easy," Chris boasted. "My father when he is a young man, he goes down two hundred feet with just a stone to make him sink fast, and a rope to pull him up again. He stays under three whole minutes without breathing."

Chris's face clouded. "But he dives too long," he said. "And he gets sick. But some day I find treasure, take my father home, get a little boat in Greece and be a fisherman myself."

Chris's smile came back. "Got to get busy. Keep looking if I wish to find treasure," he said. He hesitated, then added, "Maybe I take you

60

with me tomorrow if you like to go? Nice fun even if we find nothing."

"That would be great!" Bob said. "If we aren't needed, that is."

"We might have to do something for the movie company," Jupiter added. "Or practise diving some more."

Then he surprised them, and himself, by giving a mighty sneeze.

"Are you catching cold, Jupe?" Bob asked.

"Do not dive if you have cold!" Chris warned. "Ears hurt fierce. Well, so long, I must get busy. See you tomorrow, maybe."

He let go, hoisted his sail, and in a moment the little boat was skimming across the sunlit surface of the bay.

A few minutes later, Pete and Jeff Morton surfaced and climbed aboard. Pete shucked off his gear, grinning widely.

"It was terrific," he said. "Had a little trouble clearing my eustachian tubes, but I swallowed hard and that fixed them up. Now it's your turn, Jupe."

Jupe got ready a little less eagerly than the others. Jupe was not naturally athletic, and though he liked swimming all right, he was not really keen on it. When he was ready and had passed Jeff Morton's inspection, he and Jeff slipped over the side.

"Bob!" Pete said excitedly as the other two vanished under the water. "Guess what?"

"What?" Bob asked.

"I think I saw something. Just as we were turning to come up, I saw something gleaming on the sand about fifty feet from the sunken yacht. I'll bet it's a gold doubloon. If we dive again I'm going to try to find it!"

"Wow, are you sure?"

"Not positive. I just got a glimpse of something bright. But it could be. Everybody says there's treasure scattered loose all over the bottom of this bay."

Bob started to reply, then stopped. Jeff Morton and Jupiter were already coming back up! In fact, Jeff was helping Jupiter, who was swimming blindly, his face mask twisted to one side of his face.

"What happened?" Bob asked.

"Nothing to be alarmed at," Jeff said. "Somehow Jupiter knocked his face mask loose. I don't know how but we weren't down far and he didn't lose his air hose."

The two climbed aboard, Jupiter looking miserable.

"My ears hurt as we went down," he said. "I tried to swallow to open the eustachian tubes. Then I had to sneeze. I pulled out my mouthpiece and held it, but I had to move my face mask to sneeze and I couldn't put it back again and—well, I guess I didn't do too well," he finished miserably.

He sneezed again.

"You're catching a cold," Jeff said sternly. "You should never have tried to dive today. Lucky we were only down a few feet. No more diving for you, my boy, for the next few days!"

"No sir, I guess not," Jupiter said humbly. "The air conditioning on the plane yesterday was pretty chilly and then being out in the storm last night—well, I guess I'm catching a cold all right."

"Never dive unless you're in excellent health," Jeff said. "Especially not if you have a cold or cough. Well, I'm supposed to give you kids practice in diving and I'll go ahead with Bob and Pete, but if you're going to be laid up, we may have to change our plans."

For the next couple of hours, Bob and Pete alternated in longer and longer dives. By the end of the afternoon they felt weary, but were sure they could handle any simple underwater diving that might be required of them.

On each dive, Bob kept his eyes open for the shiny thing Pete said he'd seen, but he didn't spot it. On the last dive of the day, though, Pete came up with his right hand tightly clenched. He scrambled aboard and hastily removed his face mask and mouthpiece.

"Look!" he said exultantly.

He opened his fist. On his palm lay a worn but shiny round coin, large and heavy.

"Holy cats!" Jeff exclaimed. "A doubloon!" He examined it carefully. "Dated 1712, and

Spanish, all right. Pete, whatever you do, don't let anybody know about this. I mean, besides us and your father."

"Why not?" Pete asked, puzzled. "You mean someone would try to take it away from me?"

"No, it's yours all right, you found it on the open sea bottom. But the people around here are treasure happy! They know in their hearts that there isn't any gold on Skeleton Island, but if word got round that you'd found something, the treasure hunters would be swarming over the island in no time. They'd ruin any chance we have of ever getting that movie finished!"

9

Mrs. Barton has Suspicions

THE BOYS were ready for bed early that night. Pete and Bob were weary from their diving, and Jupe was feeling very droopy because of the cold he was catching.

Mr. Crenshaw came to Mrs. Barton's home and had dinner with them. He was worried about the progress of the work on Skeleton Island.

"That story of the phantom of the merry-go-round is all around town!" he exclaimed angrily. "Tom Farraday has been telling people the truth, but they'd rather believe in a ghost than the truth. Oh, well, we'll make out somehow. I'll see you boys in the morning. Have to go now and try to line up a couple of new carpenters."

After he had left, they went to their room. They examined the gold doubloon repeatedly. It was very exciting to have a piece of pirate treasure in their hands, even knowing they'd probably not see any more. Then Pete put it under his pillow and they turned in.

They all slept soundly until Mrs. Barton called them for breakfast.

"Come and get it, boys!" she sang out up the stairs. "Pete, your father is here. He wants to see you all before he gets started."

They scrambled into their clothes and hurried downstairs. Mr. Crenshaw was waiting, looking rushed.

"Boys," he said, "you'll have to be on your own today. I have some workmen coming so I'll be very busy. And there can't be any more diving until we get our plans straightened out. Anyway, Jeff tells me you have a cold, Jupiter, and can't dive for several days."

"Yes, sir," said Jupiter and sneezed explosively. "I'm sorry, sir." He blew his nose, which was red. "I couldn't help it."

"No, of course not." Mr. Crenshaw examined

65

him keenly. "Boy," he said, "you stay quiet for a day or so. Go over this morning and see the doctor. Name's Doctor Wilbur. Fine fellow. In fact, he's the owner of Skeleton Island. While you're eating, I'll phone him."

The boys sat down at the table, and Mrs. Barton bustled in with pancakes and sausages. Mr. Crenshaw went off to the phone and came back to tell Jupiter that Doctor Wilbur would see him at lunch-time, when he'd have a few minutes free. He wrote down the address of Doctor Wilbur's office and hurried off.

"Gosh, Jupe, it's too bad you're going to be laid up," Pete sympathized. "I was thinking maybe we could borrow the motor-boat and go exploring."

"It will give me time to think," Jupiter said, trying not to act sorry for himself. "There is much to think about. The secret of Skeleton Island, for instance. I'm sure it does have a secret, but I cannot quite fathom what it is."

"Skeleton Island!" Mrs. Barton exclaimed, as she came in with more pancakes. "That horrible place! Did you know the ghost was seen riding the merry-go-round again just night before last?"

"Yes, ma'am," Jupiter answered. "Except that there is a perfectly natural explanation." He told Mrs. Barton what had really happened.

"Well, maybe," she conceded, but she didn't look convinced. "But everybody says there's a ghost and I say, where there's so much smoke, there's bound to be some fire."

With that she went out again. Jupiter sighed.

"Mrs. Barton is a good example of the difficulty of convincing people to give up a cherished belief," he said.

Just then there was a tap at the window. They turned. A tanned face was peering in at them.

"It's Chris!" Bob exclaimed. He hurried to the door.

"I'm getting ready to go hunting again," Chris said. "You want to come with me?"

"You bet!" Bob exclaimed. "Pete and I can. Jupiter has a bad cold."

"Too bad," Chris said. "But boat is pretty small for four anyway. I see you down at the waterfront. Bring swim trunks!"

He hurried off. When Bob told the others what Chris had wanted, Pete's face lit up.

"Great!" he said. "Maybe I'll find another doubloon! Let's go and get our trunks, Bob."

"Sure," Bob answered. "Golly, Jupe, it's too bad you can't go."

Jupe's face said he thought so, too, but the First Investigator just said stoically, "Well, if I can't, I can't. You two go on. I'll see you later."

"We'll be back for lunch."

Bob and Pete got their swimming trunks from their room. Then they hurried down to the waterfront where Chris had his sailing-boat tied to an old sagging pier. They jumped in, and they were off on their first hunt for pirate treasure!

Left alone, Jupiter sighed a couple of times. Then, deciding to make the best of it, he went up to look again at Bob's notes and the magazine articles about Skeleton Island.

Mrs. Barton was in their room making the beds.

"Just thought I'd slip up and straighten your room while you boys were eating," she said. "I— land's sake, what's this?"

She had picked up Pete's pillow, and there was the gold doubloon.

"Land's alive!" the woman exclaimed. "It's an old Spanish gold piece. Treasure!"

She looked at Jupiter with wide eyes. "You boys found it out on Skeleton Island yesterday, I'll be bound. Didn't you, now?"

"Pete found it," Jupiter said. He remembered that Jeff Morton had warned them not to let anyone know of the find. But now the cat was out of the bag.

"He didn't find it on the island, though, but in the water. Quite a way from the island," Jupiter added.

"My, my!" Mrs. Barton clucked, finishing the bed. "On his very first day here, too."

She gave Jupiter a shrewd glance.

"You know," she said, "lots of folks are saying this business about making a movie out on Skeleton Island is just—well, just a big story. They say you folks are really hunting for old

Captain One-Ear's treasure that was never found. They say you have a new map and everything."

"That might explain why the company is being bothered," Jupiter said thoughtfully. "If people think there is a treasure map, they might be prowling around hoping to find it. And they might be trying to drive the movie company away in order to look for the treasure themselves.

"But really, Mrs. Barton, we don't know a thing about any treasure. All we want to do is get a few scenes of a new movie shot. You can tell everybody that."

"Well, I'll do that," Mrs. Barton answered. "But I don't know as they'll believe me. Once they get an idea in their heads it's a sightly job to shake it out again."

"Yes," Jupiter agreed. "Like they keep on believing in the ghost. Do you mind if I ask you some questions, Mrs. Barton? You've lived here all your life, and you can probably tell me a lot."

"Lands, I don't mind." The woman laughed. "Let me finish this room, then I'll come downstairs and have a cup of coffee and you can ask me any questions you like."

Jupe took Bob's bundle of notes downstairs and read them until Mrs. Barton joined him, sipping a cup of black coffee.

"Now ask away, boy," she said.

"Tell me how Skeleton Island came to be

haunted in the first place, Mrs. Barton," he requested, by way of getting started. Of course, he had read the story already, but he wanted to see if the local version agreed.

With great animation Mrs. Barton started talking. What she said tallied closely with what Jupe had read. However, the woman had more to add. After Pleasure Park had been abandoned, she said, the ghost stopped appearing. Then suddenly, some years back, it had appeared again—not just once, but several times a year.

"These fishermen who saw it," Jupiter asked, pinching his lip, "were they reliable men? People you could believe?"

"Well, now." Mrs. Barton frowned slightly. "I don't know as they were exactly that. We have some pretty rough elements among our fishermen. But lands, why would anyone make up stories about seeing a ghost?"

Jupiter had no idea. Yet he couldn't help wondering if someone hadn't done just that— made up stories.

"About when did this happen?" he asked.

Mrs. Barton couldn't remember exactly. Ten years ago, or maybe fifteen. Somewhere along there. She only knew that ever since, the island had had a very bad reputation, and people rarely went there.

"Until you Hollywood folks turned up, right out of the blue," Mrs. Barton finished, eyeing

Jupiter shrewdly. "And the phantom rides the merry-go-round again and one of you boys finds a gold piece and your people talk of thieves taking their equipment and—everything. If you ask me, there's something mighty strange going on that we don't know about."

Jupiter agreed with that. All his instincts as an investigator told him something strange was going on. But for the life of him he couldn't figure out what.

10

Disaster!

THE LITTLE sailing-boat moved briskly along, heeling over under a nice breeze. The boys had the bay to themselves, with no other boats in sight except far to the south.

Soon they were docking at the pier on Skeleton Island. It was Pete's idea to ask Jeff Morton for permission to borrow two sets of Scuba equipment. They would have borrowed a set for Chris, too, but they knew Jeff wouldn't have agreed. Besides, Chris wasn't experienced in using Scuba equipment.

Jeff said they could take some equipment for practice diving, warned them not to try anything dangerous, and hurried off in the direction of Pleasure Park.

Pete and Bob got their face masks, flippers and other equipment from the locker in the motor-boat. As an afterthought they added two underwater flashlights. Then they rejoined Chris in the sailing-boat. Chris had his own face mask and was confident he could dive as well with it as they could with all their aqualung equipment.

The boys relaxed in the warm sunshine, lulled by the gentle bobbing of the boat. After a time Bob saw they were heading towards the small island known as The Hand, where they had been so mysteriously marooned on their first night.

The Hand was about a quarter of a mile long and several hundred yards across. Now by daylight they could see that it was rocky and barren, uninhabitable. Bob looked for the spout of water they had seen that first night, but there was no sign of it.

He mentioned it to Chris. The Greek boy explained that the water was too quiet today. It only happened when the wind was blowing and the waves were rolling across the bay.

"Some kind of hole under island," he said. "Waves rush in there, blow out spout. Like whale."

He sailed up to within a hundred yards of the mid-part of the island. Then he dropped sail and flung a small anchor overboard.

"Have to anchor out here," he said. "Low tide

now, rocks are too close to surface. Only at high tide boat can sail right up to the island."

With the boat bobbing at anchor, Pete and Bob put on their Scuba equipment and Chris produced an old but serviceable face mask. They eased themselves into the water. Chris swam about fifty feet, then stood up. The water was only knee-deep.

"See?" he said. "Rocky reef here. Come on."

They swam over, found rock under them, and stood on a ledge about five yards wide. On the island side was a little bay with a sandy bottom, about twenty feet deep where they were. The bright sun showed the bottom quite clearly.

"In this bay I find two doubloons at one time last week," Chris said. "The other one I find near where you dive yesterday. Maybe we are very lucky today, find some more here."

They lowered themselves off the reef and Bob and Pete inspected the bottom, while Chris swam on the surface, peering down. They saw seaweed-covered rocks, starfish, and schools of small fish. There were lots of crabs going about their business in curious sideways motion. But nothing that looked like any treasure.

Pete signalled and he and Bob rose to the surface.

"This water isn't very deep," Pete said, removing his mouthpiece. "I don't think we should waste our air here. We may want to try

73

somewhere else later. Let's take off the tanks and just use face masks, like Chris."

Bob agreed. They paddled to shore, stowed their Scuba equipment among the rocks, and swam back out to Chris. Then the three of them covered the entire length of the small bay, peering sharply down for the glint of gold.

They were not rewarded by any exciting discovery, however, and after a time they paddled in to shore to rest, warm themselves in the sun, and talk.

"Today no luck, I guess," Chris said, a bit disheartened. "I sure hope we find something. Father, he is more sick, needs care. Well, I know another place, I find gold piece once a long time ago. We go there and—"

He paused, staring at something offshore. Then all three of them became aware of the sound of a powerful motor in the distance.

A large dark-grey motor-boat, old and rather shabby, was heading towards the little cove at high speed.

"Somebody sees us, they come to hunt, too," Chris said.

Then, as the boat did not slacken speed, he leaped to his feet.

"They crash on the reef!" he cried. "Hi!" he shouted, waving his hands. "Sheer off! You hit the rocks!" Bob and Pete joined him, waving and yelling.

They could see a man in the stern of the boat,

"Sheer off!" they cried, signalling desperately.

an old hat pulled down over his face. Whether he understood their warning or not, they couldn't tell. But abruptly the roar of the motor changed. The boat slowed as if the motor had been thrown into reverse.

At the same time the bow swung round. Still with plenty of speed, the turning boat crunched into the side of Chris's anchored sailing-boat.

The heavy prow of the motor-boat cut into the smaller boat as if it were made of cardboard. For an instant the two boats were locked together. Then the man in the motor-boat gave his engine a surge of power. It reversed and pulled free.

The next thing they knew the motor-boat was heading back into open water.

The three boys stopped yelling. With sinking hearts they watched Chris's sailing-boat settle deep into the water and go under, disappearing from sight.

"Golly!" Pete groaned. "There go our clothes, our watches, everything!"

"There goes our ride home!" Bob said in dismay. "We're stranded here. Stranded again!"

Chris said nothing. Only his clenched hands and anguished face said what it meant to have lost the only thing he owned, the little sailing-boat with which he had been desperately hunting for treasure to help his father.

11

A Warning to Jupiter

JUPITER was still engrossed in Bob's notes about Skeleton Island when Mrs. Barton came to tell him lunch was ready.

"My gracious, where are Pete and Bob?" she asked. "I've fixed lunch for them, too, and they aren't anywhere in sight!"

Jupiter blinked. Bob and Pete had said they'd be back for lunch. But they'd probably got interested in searching for doubloons and forgotten the time.

"They'll be along any minute," he said. "I'll eat now. I have to go and see Doctor Wilbur soon."

Jupiter had a sandwich and a glass of milk at a scrubbed pine table in the kitchen. His nose was running badly and he still wasn't very hungry. Mrs. Barton told him how to get to Doctor Wilbur's clinic, which was only a few blocks away.

Not many people were on the streets. He walked past rows of colonial-style houses, many of which needed paint badly. He also passed a number of vacant stores with "For Rent" signs in the windows. Empty stores are usually a good sign that a town is having hard times, and business in Fishingport seemed very bad indeed.

Doctor Wilbur's clinic was a neat brick building, fairly new. In the waiting room was a woman with two small children, and two elderly men who sat patiently looking ahead of them at nothing.

The nurse behind the desk sent Jupiter straight in. He found himself in a combination office and examination room, with a desk at one end, and an examining table and white cabinet full of medicines at the other.

Doctor Wilbur, a tall man with greying hair, sat at his desk eating a sandwich.

"Hello, Jupiter," he said, eyeing the stocky First Investigator keenly. "I'll be right with you."

He took a swallow of coffee from a thermos and stood up. Rapidly and efficiently, he examined Jupiter's nose, throat and ears, listened to his heartbeat, tapped his chest, and took his blood pressure.

"Mmm," he said a few minutes later. "You seem to have a bad cold. Probably the sudden change of climate from California."

He got some white pills from the medicine cabinet, put them in an envelope and handed them to Jupiter.

"Take two of these every four hours for the next two days," he said. "Get plenty of rest and

78

stay out of the water. I'm sure you'll feel a lot better soon."

"Excuse me, sir," Jupiter said, "can you spare me enough time for a few minutes' talk? I mean, if you're not too busy——"

"Have to finish my lunch," the doctor said, giving him another sharp look. "We can talk until then." He crossed to his desk and sat down again.

"All right, shoot," he said. "What do you want to talk about?"

"Well, I'm just trying to get all the information I can," Jupiter said. "Since you own Skeleton Island, where the movie company has been having so much trouble——"

"Skeleton Island!" Doctor Wilbur exclaimed. "I'm getting sick of hearing the name! That poor Sally Farrington was too nice a girl ever to become a ghost!"

"Then you don't believe in the ghost these fishermen say they've seen?" Jupiter asked.

"I do not. Those fishermen are an ignorant, superstitious lot. The ghost was seen just exactly once, and I can tell you the truth of that occasion. It was a silly practical joke by some very foolish pranksters. I was a young man at the time—the island belonged to my father—and I made it my business to find out. I know who it was—three boys who have since moved away.

"They rowed out to the island, started up the

merry-go-round, and one of them put on a white sheet. They waited until the lights and music had attracted investigators from town, then they left, rowing away in the darkness on the far side of the island.

"However, they never would admit it and I couldn't prove it. I told people it had been a prank, but everyone preferred to believe in the phantom. Ghosts are much more exciting to believe in than practical jokers!"

Jupiter nodded. Doctor Wilbur's story sounded like the truth.

"Once a wild story like that gets started," the doctor said, "you can never kill it. From time to time thereafter people claimed to have seen the phantom. The story was partly responsible for Pleasure Park's closing, but only partly. The truth is, another amusement park was built near Melville, and it was newer and more convenient. My father didn't have the money to compete with it, so eventually he had to close.

"When he died, I inherited the island. I couldn't sell it and there was no point in re-opening the park, so I've simply let it sit there.

"It's never made me a cent, all these years, until you people came along and offered to rent it for your movie. If—" and Doctor Wilbur looked at Jupiter from beneath bushy eyebrows —"you really *are* making a movie. People seem to think you have a clue to a vast pirate treasure hidden on the island, and are hunting for it."

"No, sir." Jupiter shook his head. "That's just a story, like the story about the ghost."

"Hmph! I rather hoped it was true, because if you found any treasure it would probably belong to me, being on my island."

"No, sir. We're not looking for treasure. Everybody says any treasure hidden there was found years ago."

"Of course it was. And I believe you. But people aren't rational about treasure. They'll believe anything."

"Doctor Wilbur," Jupiter asked, "why do you think some of the local people are trying to keep us from making a movie on your island? Because that's what I think is happening."

"Hmph!" the doctor said again and poured himself some more coffee. "If they think there's treasure, they're trying to chase you away before you find it. Or they may just be trying to steal some of your equipment—you know, many folks around here are terribly poor since the oyster fishing went bad. Or, it might be the mean streak some of the fishing people have. They may think it fun to plague you Hollywood people. Three possible reasons—take your choice."

"It seems hard to understand," Jupiter said, frowning.

"Trying to solve the mystery, eh?" The doctor smiled. "Understand you're sort of a whiz of a boy detective."

"I wouldn't say that, sir," Jupiter answered modestly, though he did have a pretty good opinion of himself. "My friends and I have done some detection. Here's our card."

He handed Doctor Wilbur one of The Three Investigators' business cards. It read:

THE THREE INVESTIGATORS

"We Investigate Anything"

?   ?   ?

First Investigator - JUPITER JONES
Second Investigator - PETER CRENSHAW
Records and Research - BOB ANDREWS

"The question marks," Jupiter explained, "are our symbol. They stand for questions unanswered, mysteries unsolved, enigmas of all sorts that we attempt to unravel."

Doctor Wilbur smiled.

"Pretty highfalutin'," he remarked. "But I like to see a boy with confidence in himself. Tell me, why do you suppose Sam Robinson deliberately marooned you on The Hand when you got here?"

"To scare us, I think," Jupiter said. "To make us want to go back to Hollywood. Because

82

somebody is afraid we might find out the reason why the movie company is being bothered so. That makes the mystery even bigger, sir. It can't be mere mischief."

"Mmm." Doctor Wilbur shot him another keen glance. "You have a point there, son. You're smarter than you look."

"Thank you. Tell me, sir, I understand that stories about the ghost of the merry-go-round died out for many years, then suddenly began again ten or fifteen years ago. Can you tell me just when?"

"Let me see now—" the doctor stroked his chin—"I began to hear them just after I moved into this building. That was about ten years ago. Yes, that would be it. The ghost stories started up ten years ago and have been pretty thick ever since, at least among the more uneducated people in town. Why do you want to know?"

"I'm not sure," Jupiter confessed, "but anything might be important, sir. Thank you very much. I guess I've taken up enough of your time."

"Not at all." The doctor stood up. "Going to be very interested if you find any answers. And," he called after Jupiter, "if there's any treasure on that island, remember it belongs to me!"

Jupiter went out in a thoughtful mood. He had learned some things but he wasn't sure yet just what they meant. It would take a lot of thinking.

As he stepped out on the street, a passing car stopped and backed up. Chief Nostigon was driving it.

"Hello, boy," the chief said. "Thought you'd like to know we traced that scoundrel Sam Robinson. He's skipped."

"Skipped?" Jupiter asked.

"Got a job as a deck hand on a freighter, sailed out this morning. Won't be back for months, if ever. Did say, though, one friend reports, he did it just for a joke. Because you lads came here with such big reputations. Can't say I swallow that."

"I don't either," Jupiter answered.

"Well, that's all we've learned," the chief said. "I'll be in touch with you folks if we get anything more." And he drove off.

Jupiter continued towards Mrs. Barton's boarding house in a thoughtful frame of mind. He felt sure he should be able to guess the answer to the curious mystery of Skeleton Island, but so far it eluded him.

He hardly noticed his surroundings until, as he was passing a tavern, a tall, thin man stepped out in front of him and barred his way. Jupiter had to stop to avoid bumping into him.

"Hold on a second there, kid," the thin man said, his face twisting in an ugly grin. "I want to give you some advice."

"Oh? Yes, sir?" Jupiter recognized that the man was unfriendly, and he let his round face go slack so that he looked—as he could when he wanted to—very stupid.

"Just take a tip from me. Go back to Hollywood where you belong if you want to keep a whole skin. And take the rest of those movie fellows along with you. None of you are wanted here in Fishingport."

The man continued to grin nastily and Jupiter saw a tattoo mark on the back of his hand. It wasn't too clear, but it looked like a mermaid. He felt a little shiver of fear run down his spine.

"Yes, sir," he said, keeping a dull expression. "I'll tell them that. Who shall I say gave me the message?"

"Never mind the wise stuff, kid!" the man snapped. "Just vamoose if you know what's good for you. That's my helpful hint for today!"

Abruptly he stepped back into the tavern.

Jupiter's heart stopped beating quite so fast. Slowly, he walked on towards Mrs. Barton's. It certainly seemed he'd been right about one thing. Someone was very determined to drive the movie company away from Skeleton Island.

12

An Exciting Discovery

"My boat!" Chris was fighting hard to keep back tears. "It is gone. No more boat. No more chance to find treasure."

"Gosh, yes," Bob said, realizing Chris's loss was much greater than theirs. "What got into that guy anyway? Was it an accident or did he do it on purpose?"

"On purpose!" Chris said angrily. "Or else he would stop, see who owned boat, say he is sorry!"

"I suppose so," Bob said. "But why on earth would anybody want to wreck your boat, Chris?"

"Keep me from hunting treasure," Chris said. "Lots of fishermen don't like me. Don't like any strangers. Think the bay, the whole place belongs to them."

They stood there a moment longer, unable to decide what to do. They were hungry, there were no other boats in sight, and no way to signal. How long would they have to stay there?

"Well, anyway," Bob said at last, "we didn't lose the Scuba equipment. It's pretty valuable and I'd hate to have to pay for it."

"Gosh, yes!" Pete said. "This kind of equipment costs hundreds of dollars and—wait a minute!"

He and Bob looked at each other, the same idea coming to them in the same instant.

"Why, we can dive down for our clothes!" they exclaimed together.

Chris grinned, shaking off his gloom.

"We all can dive!" he said. "I am the son of

Greek sponge fisherman. I bet I can dive better than you, even if I don't stay down so long."

Now excitement spurred them on. Bob and Pete got swiftly into their Scuba diving gear, and they all waded out into the bay. They swam to the reef and walked over it, then lowered themselves into the deep water beyond.

The sunken sailing-boat was a glimmer of white on the bottom, seeming to sway gently as small waves washed the surface. Bob and Pete began to propel themselves downwards with their flippered feet.

Chris had picked up a rock from the shore and, clutching it in his arms, he sank rapidly past them. He reached the sand beside the wrecked sailing-boat before they were halfway down. He rummaged inside the boat, which lay on its side, for the clothes they had stowed neatly under the seat. With his arms full, he shot upwards. They could see him grin as he went past.

In the peacefulness of the ocean depths, Bob and Pete for a moment forgot their plight. They were Scuba divers doing a real salvage job, even if only on a tiny sailing-boat.

Close together, they kicked down to the boat and grasped the side. The sail rippled in the water and they had to take care to avoid being caught in it. They examined the interior of the boat. Chris had missed a pair of pants—Bob's pants—and Bob swam a few feet to rescue them.

Pete had to dive for one of Chris's shoes that slipped away from him and began to move away along the bottom. In fact, a fairly strong current seemed to be moving the whole boat, and when they let go of the side, they had to swim to get back to it.

After five minutes, they figured they had everything that could be rescued, and Bob nodded to Pete. They kicked upwards. They broke water to see Chris standing on the reef waiting for them. He grinned as they climbed up on the rock with their salvage.

"We do not do so bad, yes?" he said. "I guess we got everything."

He took his clothing from Pete and examined the soggy bundle. Then his face fell.

"My compass is not here," he said. "Nice one. I go back down and look."

He dived into the water.

"I guess we might as well take our stuff ashore and spread it out to dry," Pete said.

"I sure wish we had some way of signalling," Bob said. "Your dad will think we were mighty careless, getting stuck on this island again."

"It wasn't our fault, or Chris's fault either," Pete said. He picked up the two heavy-duty underwater flashlights they had rescued from the sunken boat. "I'm sure glad we got these back. They're expensive. And if we have to stay until dark we can signal with them."

"Golly!" Bob looked at the sun. "It's quite a

while to dark. I hope we don't have to stay here until then. I'm starved!"

"Let's get our clothes dry, then see what we can think of," Pete suggested.

They slid their face masks into place, then eased into the water and swam to The Hand. Wringing out their clothes, they spread them flat on the warm rocks, which promised to dry them in no time. They had removed their face masks and were starting to get out of their Scuba equipment when they suddenly realized that Chris had not reappeared. They had been busy for at least ten or fifteen minutes, and Chris was still underwater.

That could only mean trouble.

"Golly!" Bob blurted out. "Something must have happened to Chris!"

"Maybe he got caught down there." Pete went pale at the thought. "We have to try to rescue him!"

Without another word they got back into their diving gear, and started paddling for the reef.

They stood on the rocky ledge a moment, staring down into the sunlit green water. No moving form that could be Chris caught their eye, nor could they see the sunken sailing-boat now. Together they shoved off into the deeper water and started propelling themselves downwards, their hearts beating fast with anxiety.

There were cavities in the base of the reef—hollows formed by the currents. Maybe Chris had been pulled into one of them and got stuck. Or could he be tangled in the sail or trapped beneath the boat?

Soon they located the boat. Underwater currents had sent it bumping along the bottom of the reef for about twenty feet. They headed for it, but Chris wasn't in the boat.

Bob swam down until he could touch the sandy bottom. He peered under the boat fearfully. But Chris wasn't there, either. Whatever had happened to him he had not got caught in the rigging. Bob knew there were no sharks in these waters, or other deadly fish. What other danger could Chris have encountered?

Pete touched his arm. He held up two fingers side by side, then pointed towards a rock formation. Bob understood. He meant they should investigate the rocks together. Underwater you always stayed close to your buddy in case of trouble. Bob nodded and they set out, kicking themselves along vigorously.

The bottom of the reef was irregular. In places, small dark hollows had been cut by the swift current. They peered into each hollow place, wishing they had brought the underwater flashlights. But all they saw were swarms of little fish that swam hastily away at their intrusion.

Seaweed made waving curtains in spots, and

they had to push it aside to peer into the water beyond. At least five minutes passed. They had covered a good hundred feet without a sign of Chris.

They paused and put their face masks close together. Bob could see Pete's eyes, wide and anxious. Bob pointed back in the other direction. Pete nodded. Side by side they kicked rapidly back towards the sunken boat. They had almost reached the sailing-boat when a swiftly swimming figure shot past them.

It was Chris, and he was in a hurry to get to the surface!

How could Chris have stayed under water for twenty minutes without any diving gear?

They headed for the surface. Chris was sitting on the edge of the reef in waist-deep water, gulping great breaths of air into his lungs. He certainly didn't look hurt, and he was grinning broadly.

They came up beside him and shoved up their face masks.

"Good grief, Chris, you gave us a scare!" Pete exclaimed.

"Where were you?" Bob asked, grinning with relief. "What happened?"

Chris threw back his head and laughed merrily.

"I find something," he said, and held up his right fist, tightly closed. "Guess what?"

"Your compass?" Bob asked.

The Greek boy shook his head. "Guess again."

"A gold piece!" Pete cried.

Still grinning, Chris opened his hand. An irregularly shaped, shiny gold blob lay in his palm. It was rather battered, but it was certainly a gold piece.

"You never guess what I find," he said.

"A treasure chest?" Bob said hopefully. "Buried in the sand?"

"No, not that. I find a round opening in the bottom of the reef. Fish swimming in and out. I think, if fish can swim, Chris can swim. I swim in."

He paused dramatically.

"I find an underwater cave under the island! I find this doubloon in it! I bet—I bet there is a lot more treasure down there!"

13

The Secret Cave

SIDE BY SIDE, Bob and Pete floated in the water about five feet from the bottom. Bubbles went up from their breathing tubes in little clusters. A school of sea bass wriggled past them and disappeared into the black opening the boys were staring at.

It was not a big opening, perhaps only twelve feet wide by four or five feet high. It was shaped roughly like an eye—a dark, staring eye without any eyeball. The sides were smooth from the water currents that went in and out with the tides, and though there was seaweed nearby, none grew in the opening of the underwater cave.

Twenty feet to one side, Chris's sunken sailing-boat bobbed a little, but Bob and Pete weren't interested in the sailing-boat at the moment. They were engrossed in this underwater cave Chris had found. Each of the boys now had one of the waterproof flashlights in his hand, and in a minute, as soon as they got up their nerve a little more, they were going to swim into the cave and explore it.

According to Chris's story there was no danger.

He had been unable to find his compass on the sandy bottom of the bay. However, just as he was about to surface, he had seen the mouth of the underwater cave. Thinking of possible treasure inside, he impulsively swam in.

The cave seemed to get bigger as he went. It was dark, but he could look back and see the light spot which was the opening, and he kept that behind him.

He had just decided to turn back when he realized that in his excitement he had gone farther than he should. He didn't have breath enough to get outside and up to the surface.

"I sure am one scared fish then." Chris had grinned when he came to this point in his story. "I know my only chance is to go ahead, maybe cave will get big and I can come up for air. I swim like crazy. Then I see little bit of light ahead of me. I swim that way, then I come up and I have air to breathe! I breathe hard, then I look round. I am in a cave under the island! A hole going up through rocks lets in enough light to show me rocky ledge, covered with seaweed. I climb out to rest. My hand touches gold piece under seaweed. I get very excited. I look under all the seaweed for more gold, but cannot find any. Then I swim out to get you."

An underwater cavern with pirate treasure in it! If Chris could swim into it without any Scuba equipment, Pete and Bob could certainly do it with the modern aqualungs they had borrowed from Jeff Morton. It didn't sound dangerous. They could certainly take a quick look anyway.

As the boys hesitated at the entrance to the cave, a white body swam between them. It was Chris. Waving to them, he shot like an arrow into the dark mouth of the cave. With one accord they followed.

The twin beams of their flashlights gave excellent illumination in the clear water. On either side rose the rocky walls of the cave, heavily fringed with seaweed. Startled fish scurried past. A green moray eel poked its heavily fanged head out of a crevice in the rock, and the boys gave it a wide berth.

Chris was out of sight, swimming much faster than they. They had to be careful not to rub against the side of the passage lest it damage or pull off some of their Scuba equipment.

Pete shone his light upwards. Suddenly the top of the tunnel vanished. The boys swam quickly up—twenty feet, thirty feet. Abruptly their masked faces popped out of the water.

They were in a sizeable cavern with a rough ceiling four or five feet above their heads. Chris was sitting on a rocky ledge, dangling his feet in the water. The two boys paddled over and climbed cautiously up beside him on the slippery seaweed. They pushed up their face masks.

"We are inside The Hand now," Chris said to them. "How do you like my cave?"

"Golly!" Bob said fervently. "I'll bet nobody but us has ever been in here!"

He flashed his light around. The cavern was irregularly shaped, the roof varying from four to six feet above the water. Down towards the far end the cave narrowed sharply. However, there was a splash of daylight there, which puzzled them for a moment.

They shut off their flashlights to study it, and in the gloomy half-light the cave began to seem much bigger, eerie and mysterious. The eddying water made little gurgling noises against the rock, and strands of seaweed rose and fell like the floating hair of some mysterious underwater creature.

"There must be a hole in the rocks, going up to the surface," Bob said, puzzled.

"The spout!" Chris exclaimed. "It's that hole, the blowhole. In storm, water comes in here, rushes against rocks, and shoots up spout. Only nobody knows there is a cave down here. Think it is just a narrow crack some place down deep!"

"Sure, that's it!" Bob cried. He remembered how they had seen the water spouting up from the middle of the island during the storm two nights before. And of course, his notes mentioned the spout as something the very first explorers had discovered. Now they had found what caused it, something no one else had ever done.

"Oh," Bob's face fell, and the others looked at him inquiringly. "I just thought of something," he said. "If we're the first people ever to find this cave, there can't be any pirate treasure hidden in it."

"I didn't think of that!" Pete groaned.

"How do we know?" Chris demanded. "I find one gold piece, don't I? Let me have the flashlight and I dive down and see!"

Bob gave him a flashlight and Chris slipped

into the water. In the darkness they could see a dim glow of light as Chris swam down to the sandy bottom.

"It sure would have been nice if this had been a secret pirate hiding place no one had found before," Pete said. "But you're probably right, Bob."

They watched the glimmer of light below them move back and forth. Chris could certainly stay down a long time! It must have been two and a half minutes before the light went out.

An instant later Chris's head popped out of the water. Pete turned on his light, and Chris climbed up next to them.

"You are right," he said in a gloomy voice. "No treasure down there. Just crabs, fish, shells. Like this."

He opened his clenched fist.

In it lay two gold doubloons!

"Wow!" Pete and Bob whooped together. "Chris! Where were they?"

"In sand," Chris said.

They passed the gold pieces eagerly from hand to hand. They felt wonderfully heavy and valuable.

"Now we got three!" Chris said, eyes shining. "One each."

"No, you found them," Bob said. "They're yours."

"Share equal," Chris said stubbornly. "Now you go down. Maybe you will find more. Maybe

97

enough to buy me a new boat, and take good care of my father!"

Eagerly, Bob and Pete adjusted their face plates, made sure their breathing tubes were in working order, and slid into the water.

The sandy bottom was dotted with shells. As they turned their lights this way and that, they saw nothing unusual. Then Pete spotted a shiny glint at the edge of the rocky wall. It was a gold doubloon, half buried in the sand.

Bob swam back and forth over the bottom with easy kicks of his flippered feet. A few minutes later he spotted a shiny object, partly hidden beneath an empty oyster shell. It, too, was a doubloon.

Excitement overwhelmed both boys. There really was pirate treasure in this underwater cave! Not handily stacked up in a nice, solid chest, maybe, but scattered over the bottom. There must be more and they would find it!

Heedless of the passage of time, they scoured the sandy bottom. They turned over oyster shells, making clouds of sand in the water and then having to wait until it cleared to search some more.

When they had found half a dozen gold doubloons each, their hands were too full to hold any more. Bob tapped Pete and they swam up and clambered out of the water. Exultantly they poured their golden find on to a flat spot on the ledge.

"We found some!" Bob said excitedly. "Chris, you're right, there *is* treasure in this cave!"

Smiling, Chris reached behind him and produced three more doubloons. "I find these on ledge under the seaweed," he said.

"I'll bet there's more!" Bob said. "I don't know where it came from, but if we found this much we ought to be able to find some more."

"You've convinced me!" Pete said. "Come on, let's keep looking."

Treasure fever makes it impossible for a person to think of anything else. And the three boys certainly had treasure fever now. Heedless of time or any other consideration, they began to search the underwater cave. They swam along the bottom inch by inch, and explored every crevice of the rocky cave.

Even as they hunted however, something was happening that they couldn't possibly guess. Chris's sunken sailing-boat, nudged by the underwater currents, was being wedged into the eye-shaped mouth of the cavern. There it stuck, sealing up the entrance like a cork in a bottle.

The three boys were trapped in an underwater cave that nobody knew existed!

A Dangerous Predicament

JUPITER was worried. It was late in the afternoon and still Bob and Pete had not come back from their sail with Chris. What could have happened to them?

He got up from the desk where he had spread out all Bob's papers and the notes he had added to them. He plucked a tissue from the large box Mrs. Barton had provided. Staring out of the window, he inspected the north end of the bay. There was no little sailing-boat in sight.

Mrs. Barton came in, bringing a glass of milk and some cookies.

"Maybe you'd like a snack, Jupiter," she said. "Lands, aren't those two boys back yet? Where can they be?"

"I don't know," Jupiter said, shaking his head. "They said they'd be back for lunch, and they're very reliable. Maybe they're in some trouble."

"Now, it doesn't pay to worry," the woman said. "Maybe they started fishing off one of the rocks and forgot the time."

She bustled out. Jupiter sat down and

munched the cookies while he looked at his notes.

In his mind he tried to sum up the facts. Twenty-five years earlier, poor Sally Farrington's death and a ridiculous joke by some boys had started the legend of a phantom on Skeleton Island. For many years it apparently hadn't been seen. Then, beginning about ten years ago, it had been reported quite often, but always by an unreliable group of fishermen. As a result, no one went to Skeleton Island.

Then the movie company had come to fix up Pleasure Park and shoot some scenes there. They had run into a campaign of theft and sabotage that Jupiter felt sure was intended to drive them away.

Were the stories of the ghost somehow connected with the harassment of the movie company, or weren't they?

Jupiter was still struggling with this question when the door opened. Jeff Morton came in, looking very upset.

"Jupiter," he said, "have you seen Chris Markos?"

"Not since breakfast," Jupiter answered. "Pete and Bob went sailing with him. They haven't come back yet."

"Sailing all day!" Jeff exclaimed, his freckled face pink with anger. "But they borrowed two sets of aqualung equipment from me this morning and said they wanted to practise diving."

His features darkened.

"Do you suppose they're out diving with that crazy Greek kid, looking for treasure?"

He and Jupiter stared at each other in growing alarm.

"We'll have to go and look for them!" Jeff said. "Something may have happened to them. If anything has, on top of what's already happened——" He didn't finish the sentence, but he looked grim. "Come on, Jupiter, let's get going!"

Jupiter forgot about his cold, forgot about the mystery, and everything else but finding Bob and Pete and Chris. He followed Jeff down to the waterfront, where a small boat with an outboard motor was tied to the pier.

They got in, the motor spun to life, and they roared out into the bay.

Jupiter wanted to ask Jeff what he had meant when he started to say "on top of what's already happened, "but he was obviously in no mood for conversation. In any case, the roar of the motor made it difficult to talk.

They sped over to the pier on Skeleton Island where the bigger motor-boat was tied up.

"We'll need more room to bring the kids back when we find them," Jeff explained as they got into the bigger boat. "Also," he added ominously, "I want my gear handy in case I have to do any diving."

That could only mean, Jupiter thought gloomily, that Jeff Morton was afraid something had happened to the boys while they were diving. He tried to put the thought out of his mind.

Bob and Pete weren't reckless. They wouldn't have any crazy accidents. But he knew that not all accidents were due to recklessness. Sometimes something unexpected just happened.

Jeff swung the powerful motor-boat out into the bay and they began their search. First Jeff circled Skeleton Island. Then he skirted up past the rocky reefs between the bigger island and The Hand. Finally he made a circle twice around The Hand.

"Nowhere in sight," he said to Jupiter, cutting the motor to idling. "That sailing-boat isn't in this part of the bay. The only other possibility I can think of is that the boys sailed over to the east side of the bay. We'll just have to go over there and cover every inch of the coastline."

Jupiter nodded. Jeff moved a lever, the motor took hold, and the boat started to roar away from The Hand.

Meanwhile, in the submerged cavern beneath The Hand, Bob, Pete and Chris crouched on the seaweed-covered ledge, dark water eddying

103

round their waists. They didn't know how long they had been in the cave. But at the end where the blowhole was, the light had faded, and the tide had risen at least two feet.

They had been too excited at first to think about anything but the gold doubloons they were finding. They had gathered between forty and fifty gold pieces, which now filled the little canvas sack Chris had brought along for treasure. It wasn't a very big fortune, it was true, but an exciting find all the same.

Suddenly Chris had realized the tide was rising.

"We better get out of here," he told them cheerfully. "Anyway, we find all the gold, I think."

"We haven't found a doubloon for at least half an hour," Pete agreed. "And I'm starved. It must be awful late."

It was Pete, in the lead, who first saw the boat jammed in the entrance. It had slid into the eye-shaped opening on its side, its mast and flapping sail inward. The movement of the water had ground it into place and caught the tip of the mast in a crack in the rock.

Pete's flashlight picked up every detail. Less than a foot of space was left between the boat and the rocks. They couldn't possibly scrape through there. They were trapped!

Together Pete and Bob swam against the boat and pushed. All they did was push themselves backwards in the water. The boat didn't budge.

At that moment Chris came shooting between them. He saw the boat at the last minute, hesitated just long enough to take in the situation, then turned and swam desperately back into the cave. He had to surface and get another breath before the air in his lungs was exhausted.

Pete and Bob suddenly remembered that their own air was running low. They made another effort to push the sailing-boat out of the way, with the same lack of success. Then they followed Chris.

A couple of minutes later they were all crouched on the ledge.

"Golly! We are in a jam!" Chris said. "Tide has that boat wedged in tight."

"It sure has," Pete agreed glumly. "Who'd ever expect a thing like that to happen?"

"I noticed the tide was moving the boat earlier," Bob put in. "But I never expected it to push it into the entrance. What are we going to do?"

There was a long silence. Then Chris said, "Tide is coming in now. Pushing boat in. Maybe when tide goes out, water will push boat out again. We must hope so, I guess."

"But the tide won't turn for hours yet!" Pete groaned. "And when it does, suppose the boat doesn't move?"

"We've got a bigger problem than that," Bob said.

"Bigger problem?" Chris repeated. "What do you mean?"

"Look." Bob flashed his light upward. Just above their heads arched the roof of the cavern, wet and slimy with seaweed.

"See?" Bob said. "When the tide rises, this cave gets full of water. If we wait for the tide to turn, we'll be under water."

The rising water gurgled as it lapped around them. Nobody had anything to say. They knew Bob was right.

At that moment, in the motor-boat that was speeding away from The Hand, Jupiter gave a yell.

"Mr. Morton!" he called. "Turn back! I see something on the shore."

Jeff Morton frowned but swung the boat round. A minute later they were nudging up on a tiny sandy beach. Jupiter was out of the boat and running along the shore towards the rocks where he had glimpsed the boys' clothes. By the time Jeff had secured the boat and joined him, Jupe was excitedly rummaging through the now dry clothing.

"All their clothes!" he told Jeff. "They must still be here somewhere. Maybe they're diving on the other side of The Hand. I'll go and see."

Jeff Morton stared at the clothes in perplexity.

"The boat isn't here!" he exclaimed. "They've left their clothes and gone off in the boat with the diving gear for some reason. We——"

But Jupiter wasn't there to listen. He was hiking up the hump in the middle of The Hand, moving much faster than he usually moved.

He reached the top of the ridge and eagerly looked down towards the other shore. For a moment he couldn't believe there was nothing in sight. He had been so positive he would see his friends, or the boat. But they weren't there.

Dismayed, and realizing now just how badly he was worried, he slumped against a boulder.

Jeff came puffing up beside him.

"We were all round this island," he said. "They aren't here, you should have known that. But where can they have gone?"

Angrily he picked up a small rock and flung it down. The rock landed in a slight hollow in front of them, rolled a bit, and went down a hole about eight inches across. After a second, there was a faint splash down below.

Jupiter hardly noticed.

"You're right," he said, "I guess we just have to try the east shore of the bay. Though I can't imagine why they'd leave their clothes here."

Jeff stood up. "Come on, we'd better get a move on. I think we should call the Coast Guard to come and help us look. It'll be dark and we'll need all the help we can get!"

Jeff started back for the motor-boat and Jupiter followed. He knew Bob and Pete and Chris were in trouble. In his imagination he could hear their voices calling for help, and he couldn't answer because he didn't know where they were. He could almost hear them, as if—

"Golly!" Jupiter whirled around and started back, his legs pumping hard. He ignored Jeff's startled shout as he ran to the little hole in the rock, the blowhole, and flung himself down beside it.

With his face directly above the hole, he shouted, "Bob! Pete! Are you down there?"

There was silence. Jupiter, his heart pounding, realized it was a crazy idea. They couldn't possibly be down under this island.

Then up out of the blowhole, muffled but clear, came Pete's answer.

"Jupe! We're in a jam! If the tide rises a little more, we'll be under water. Get us out of here!"

15

Jupiter Thinks Fast

IN THE CAVE the boys held tightly to the seaweed on the rocky ledge. Otherwise the water that was up around their shoulders would have floated them away. It was rising fast. Soon they'd have to swim and keep swimming, until the rising tide squeezed them right up against the roof.

"I wonder what's taking them so long?" Pete muttered, shivering a little. It seemed like a long time since the stone had unexpectedly come down the blowhole, and he and Bob had started yelling for help.

When they hadn't got any answer, there had been a bad minute in which they figured the rock had just rolled down by itself. But they kept on yelling, and then Jupiter's voice answered them.

After Jupiter, Jeff Morton had called down. It took a couple of minutes of yelling back and forth before they could get him to understand the situation. As soon as he realized the fix they were in, he shouted that he would get help for them fast. Then he and Jupiter went away.

Now the three boys were waiting for the promised help. Bob kept his light turned on, though the batteries were running down, because even the dim glow helped in the darkness.

"Listen!" said Chris. "We do not tell about gold doubloons. We keep that secret for now, yes?"

"Why?" Bob asked. "We'll have to explain what we were doing in here."

"Everybody with diving gear will come to

explore cave," Chris protested. "We do not get the chance to come back and look some more."

"As far as I'm concerned," Bob said, "I never want to see this cave again. I don't care how much treasure is in it. Let somebody else have it."

"I'll buy a double helping of that," Pete agreed. "Anyway, I think we found all there is. Just some doubloons that got washed in by the tide."

"But maybe there is some more!" Chris argued. "It is my big chance to find treasure to take my father back to Greece. What we have, only forty or fifty doubloons, is not nearly enough, especially when we divide up."

"Well," Bob said, "maybe we can keep it a secret. We can try, for your sake. I guess you're right about people coming to search this cave."

"Pete Crenshaw won't be among them!" Pete said fervently. "But if you want to come back, Chris, well, we'll just say we found the doubloons in the water. That's true enough. We won't say where."

"I keep doubloons secret if I can," Chris said. He clutched the canvas sack which held the coins. "I am not afraid to come back. The way we got caught would not happen again in a million years."

"Once will be enough if Jeff Morton doesn't hurry!" Pete groaned. "Golly, do you suppose he's going to have to go all the way to get the Coast Guard?"

"He'll need some help to get that sailing-boat out of the mouth of the cave," Bob said. "I'm almost sure he can't drag it loose by himself."

"But that could take a couple of hours!" Pete exclaimed, grabbing at the seaweed as a surge of water almost washed them from their slippery perch. "The tide will be in and this cave will be full by then!"

"Jupe will think of something," Bob said hopefully. "You can't beat Jupe in an emergency."

"I hope you are right," Chris said, in a very low voice. "But it sure is taking a long time!"

Actually, it had been only fifteen minutes since Jeff Morton and Jupiter had left the blowhole above and hurried back to the motor-boat. Now the boat was idling a hundred feet offshore, with Jupiter handling the controls while Jeff got as swiftly as he could into an aqualung outfit.

"Crazy kids!" he muttered, as he strapped on his weights and prepared to step over the side of the boat. "How in the dickens could they get into such a fix?"

He turned to Jupiter.

"All right, Jupiter, hold the boat steady right here," he said. "I'm going down and see what the situation is. Probably I can ease the sailing-boat out of the way. Anyway, I hope so. I don't want to have to go for the Coast Guard."

He pulled his face mask into place, grabbed an underwater flashlight, and went over the side.

Jupiter felt very much alone. In the distance he could see boats heading for Fishingport from the south end of the bay, but none came anywhere near him. The minutes went by very slowly as he waited for Jeff to come up again. When it seemed like an hour, he looked at his wristwatch and saw that only five minutes had passed. Another five minutes went by. Then Jeff Morton's head popped up right beside the boat. He climbed aboard, looking grey and anxious.

"That boat is jammed in the cave entrance, all right," he said. "As neat as a cork in a bottle. I got a grip on it and pulled but I couldn't budge it. It's a job for the Coast Guard. We'll need divers with crowbars either to break up the sailing-boat or pry it out of there."

Jupiter stared at him.

"Won't that take too long?" he asked tensely. "I mean, a couple of hours, perhaps?"

Jeff nodded slowly.

"All of that," he said. "I know what you're thinking. The cave will be full of water by then. But I don't know what else to do. If that blowhole was big enough, we could lower a line down it and pull them up. But it isn't."

Jupiter was pinching his lip, which always
112

helped him think. Now an idea was coming to him.

"Mr. Morton!" he exclaimed. "Maybe we could pull the sailing-boat loose!"

"Pull it loose?" Jeff frowned at him. "How?"

"With the motor-boat!" Jupiter said. "It has a powerful motor. We have an anchor and plenty of rope. We could hook the anchor on to the sailing-boat. Then if we give the motor full power straight ahead——"

"I'm with you!" Jeff exclaimed. "By George, it might work. Come on, we have to move fast!"

Working swiftly, he untied the anchor rope from the bow, brought it back and attached it to a ring-bolt on the stern. Then he dropped the anchor overboard, paying out all the rope.

"There!" he said. "A hundred feet of rope should be enough. Now I'm going back down to attach the anchor to the sailing-boat. When I tug on the anchor rope three times, ease the boat forward until the rope is taut. Then slowly give it full power. I'll be down there trying to help ease the sailing-boat out.

"If you feel a give, followed by a slow heavy drag, that'll mean you have the sailing-boat loose. Pull forward a hundred feet or so, then cast loose the anchor rope and reverse to come back to position. I'll swim into the cave and get those kids out.

"If you feel a tug, then suddenly you jerk free, you'll know the anchor came loose. Stop and

wait for me to come up. But pray your idea
works the first time!"

Jeff climbed over the side and was gone into
the depths again. Jupiter waited. his heart
beating anxiously, the anchor rope in his hand.
He felt a pull on it, but that was only Jeff
recovering the anchor and carrying it back to
the cave. A minute passed, two—then he felt
three sharp tugs on the rope.

Jupiter moved the boat ahead until the
anchor rope was a taut, straight line from the
stern down into the water. Then, ever so easily,
he increased the power.

The motor began to roar. The propeller threw
up a wash behind him. But the motor-boat did
not move. Jupiter increased power, his heart in
his throat for fear the anchor would tear
through the side of the sailing-boat.

Very, very slowly, the motor-boat began to
move. Sluggishly, as if pulling a whale, it gained
distance. It was dragging a dead weight across
the bottom, and it had barely enough power to
move it. But it did move. Twenty feet—fifty feet
—a hundred feet!

Jupiter would have cheered if he had not been
so intent on the job. He threw the motor
controls into neutral, and with his prized Swiss
pocket-knife reached back and cut the anchor
rope. The rope slithered down into the water.
Jupiter gave the motor reverse power and eased
back into position.

He tried to imagine what was happening below. The cave entrance was open now. Jeff was swimming in. He had found the three boys. Now he was instructing them to swim out and surface. In a minute—or two minutes—

A head popped out of the water just behind the boat. It was Chris Markos. He thrust up his face mask and breath exploded from his lungs. He paddled over to the motor-boat, grabbed on to it and pushed something heavy over the side. It dropped at Jupiter's feet with a clink.

"Hide it, Jupe!" Chris gasped. "We find treasure. But we keep it a secret. For now, anyway. Tell you all about everything later."

Jupiter hid the wet bag the best way he could think of. He sat on it.

"Boy!" said Chris when he was safely in the motor-boat. "We are sure afraid you can't get us out in time. Pete and Bob, they will be up any second."

Just then Bob's head appeared, and a second later, Pete's.

"It sure was good to hear your voice down there," said Pete when both boys had clambered aboard. "Yours and Jeff Morton's."

"He's pretty angry at us," Bob said. "I guess he has a right to be."

"When he talks to Dad, Dad will be angry, too," Pete said dolefully. "But anyway, we found some treasure. Did Chris tell you?"

"I'm sitting on it," Jupiter said. "You can tell me all about it later."

"I guess we're going to get a good bawling out," Bob said easing himself out of his gear. "But it actually wasn't our fault. First somebody sank Chris's sailing-boat, then——"

"Here comes Jeff Morton now," Jupiter interrupted him. "He'll want to hear what happened."

Jeff had surfaced at the stern of the motor-boat. In his hand he had the severed end of the anchor line. When Jupiter had grabbed it and attached it to the ringbolt, he swam round to the steps and climbed on board.

He removed his face plate and slowly took off his weights and air tank. Then he looked at the silently waiting boys.

"Well," he said at last, "I'm glad you boys are safe. Plenty glad. But that doesn't alter the fact that you acted recklessly and got into serious trouble."

"But—" Bob began. He was sure that if he could explain just how it all had happened, Jeff Morton would see that there wouldn't have been any danger except for the freakish current that had wedged the boat into the cave entrance.

Jeff held up his hand. "I don't care what your explanations are," he said. "Facts are facts. When I tell Harry Norris and Mr. Crenshaw what's happened, I'm sure they'll agree with me that you kids aren't to do any more diving.

"Hide it, Jupe!" Chris gasped.

"It was a bad idea to begin with—the water in this bay isn't really clear enough to get good underwater pictures. Harry Norris agrees with me, and I'm sure Mr. Denton will when he gets back here. So that idea of a short subject showing you diving for treasure is washed up."

He paused for breath, but it was plain he had more to say.

He turned and faced Chris.

"However," he said grimly, "I think one source of our troubles is ended. We've discovered who's been tampering with our equipment, stealing things, and giving us such a headache. Last night the equipment trailer was broken into through a small window, too small for anybody but a boy to get through. Someone stole two lenses worth almost a thousand dollars. I discovered the lenses missing—and I found something else. Something the thief dropped by accident."

His eyes bored into Chris's.

"I found your knife, Chris," he said. "Where you dropped it when you stole those lenses. Nobody else but you could have slipped through that tiny window.

"I've already reported the facts to Chief Nostigon, and when we get back to Fishingport, I'm marching you down to the police station. I'm very much afraid that you're going to jail!"

16

Jupiter Solves One Mystery

"Boy, we sure are in the doghouse!" Bob sighed.

"We're in the doghouse, but Chris is in jail," Pete said gloomily. "I don't think he stole those camera lenses, do you, Jupe?"

Jupiter didn't answer. He was sitting on the sofa in Mrs. Barton's living room, a far-away "thinking" look on his face. It was the middle of the afternoon and outside a heavy rain was pouring down. The boys had been ordered not to leave the house by Mr. Crenshaw, who had given them a severe lecture about irresponsibility the previous evening.

"Jupe!" said Pete more loudly. "I just said I don't believe Chris stole those camera lenses. Do you?"

Jupiter coughed. His cold was still bothering him.

"No," he said, "I don't. One kid can generally tell when another kid is sneaky and Chris isn't sneaky. It's just that appearances are against him. His knife being found at the scene of the crime is very peculiar."

119

"He lost it two days ago," Bob pointed out. "He said so."

"And of course the men wouldn't believe him," Jupiter said, coughing again. "They want to think the mystery of Skeleton Island is solved, so they believe he did it. That's the way adults often are."

"Well, what *is* the secret anyway?" Bob grumbled. "We're investigators and we ought to be able to at least make a guess."

"The secret is, someone wants to keep everybody away from Skeleton Island, that's all," Jupe told them. "I figured that out yesterday. The mystery is, why?"

Just then Mrs. Barton came into the room to answer the doorbell, and Jupe fell silent. Chief Nostigon came in, his raincoat dripping.

"Hello, boys," he said. "Mrs. Barton, I'd like to talk to these lads if you don't mind."

"Of course not, Chief." She went back out to the kitchen and the chief hung up his raincoat and took a seat. Deliberately he lit a cigar.

"Boys," he said, "I don't mind telling you things look bad for your friend Chris. We made a search and found those stolen camera lenses in a little woodshed behind the shanty where he lives with his father."

"He didn't steal them!" Bob said hotly. "We know he didn't!"

"Maybe not," Chief Nostigon agreed. "But the evidence is all against him. Everybody

120

knows he's trying hard to raise money to get his father back to Greece."

"He doesn't have to steal to do it!" Pete exclaimed. "He has money! And the chances are he'll find some more!"

"Oh." The chief gave them a long look. "Now that's very interesting. He has money, has he? And he may find more. Meaning just what?"

Pete, realizing he had given away the secret of the doubloons, was silent.

"Boys," the chief continued, "I like Chris and I want to help him. Now, nobody will tell me exactly what happened yesterday. Just that you kids got into some trouble and had to be rescued. I think I understand why you're keeping it such a secret. If you found some treasure and the word gets round, Skeleton Island will be swamped with treasure hunters in no time.

"Just the same, I think you ought to tell me. Maybe I can help young Chris. So suppose you give me the whole story."

They hesitated. Then Jupiter made up his mind.

"Yes, sir," he said. "Pete, go and get the canvas bag."

Pete went upstairs. A moment later he returned with Chris's bulging canvas sack. Pete spilled the contents out on the sofa. With a soft clinking sound, between forty and fifty shiny doubloons slid on to the cushions.

Chief Nostigon's eyes widened.

"By Jiminy!" he said. "That's real pirate treasure. And Chris found that?"

"Chris and Bob and Pete," Jupiter said. "In an underwater cave on The Hand. Chris wants to go back and look for some more. That's why we're keeping it a secret."

"Mmm." Chief Nostigon pulled at his chin. "Well, you can count on me. I won't blab."

"So you see," Bob said eagerly, "Chris wouldn't need to steal anything. He has money and may find more."

"Boys," the chief answered, "I'm afraid that doesn't prove anything. You see, these doubloons were found *after* the camera lenses were stolen. So Chris didn't know he was going to have money. That means appearances are still against him."

It was true. Bob scowled as he realized it. Pete jammed his hands into his pockets.

Jupiter coughed again. He blew his nose. Then he spoke up.

"Excuse me, Chief," he said. "I admit Mr. Crenshaw and Mr. Norris and Jeff Morton think the secret of Skeleton Island is solved—that Chris was causing all the trouble. But I'm sure they're wrong. There's someone else, someone we don't know about, behind it. There has to be. Let's look at all the facts from the beginning. Now to start with——"

At that moment Mrs. Barton came in.

"Supper, boys," she said. "Oh, I didn't know you were still talking. Well, talk as long as you like, Chief."

As she started to leave the room, the pile of gold coins on the sofa caught her attention. Her eyes widened and she bustled out. She hurried down the long hall to the telephone, and a moment later was talking in an excited whisper.

"My goodness, Ella May," she said. "What do you think? Those boys staying at my house really are here to help hunt for treasure. Why, I just saw an immense pile of gold pieces they found. Yes, they must have found them out on Skeleton Island. My goodness, I don't know how much there was but it seemed like a lot. It's probably just their share. I'll bet there's lots more out there!"

She hung up and dialled another number.

Unaware that news of their find was being broadcast to the town, the boys were still deep in conversation with Chief Nostigon.

Jupiter was outlining everything that had happened. First he mentioned the ghost scares that had kept people away from Skeleton Island for years. Then he reminded the chief of the troubles the movie company had had ever since it set up camp on Skeleton Island. He told again how he and Pete and Bob had been marooned their very first night in Fishingport.

Finally he brought up his warning of the previous day by the tall, thin man, a man with a

123

mermaid tattooed on his hand. The chief rubbed his chin.

"Could have been Bill Ballinger," he said. "Peculiar, mighty peculiar. Go on, boy."

Jupiter told of the way Chris's boat had been smashed and sunk, and finished up by saying:

"Chief Nostigon, doesn't the pattern seem pretty clear? Because there is a pattern. The pattern is to keep people away from Skeleton Island. First the ghost scares kept the local people away. Then, when the movie company came, someone tried to harass them into leaving.

"When word got out we three were coming to town, somebody must have thought we were more important than we were. They had that Sam Robinson maroon us on The Hand to scare us into going back.

"Then I was warned we weren't wanted and should go back to Hollywood. And almost at the same time, someone was sinking Chris's sailing-boat, to keep him from sailing round Skeleton Island. And if this wasn't enough, someone stole those camera lenses and dropped Chris's knife at the scene to implicate him and put him in jail.

"The whole pattern points to keeping everybody away from Skeleton Island."

"Well now," the chief said, "it does look that way. I'm going to have to turn this over in my mind. As for Chris, I'd like to let him out, and Doctor Wilbur will go bail for him, but Judge Harvey has to sign the papers and he's away on business. Can't do anything until he comes back. But I'll sure work to get him loose."

With that he said goodbye and left. Pete hurriedly put the gold doubloons back into their sack and carried them upstairs to hide under his mattress.

When he came back down again, supper was on the table. Mrs. Barton served them with a funny little knowing smile. Finally, as she brought out custard for dessert, she could keep quiet no longer.

"Aren't you naughty boys," she said reproachfully, "telling me you folks weren't on Skeleton Island to hunt for treasure."

They looked at her in surprise.

"But really, Mrs. Barton——" Jupiter began.

"I saw!" she said. "I saw the great heap of gold pieces you were showing the chief. I didn't mean to spy, but when I came into the room, there it was on the couch. I think it's very exciting."

The boys looked at each other in dismay.

"Did you tell anyone, Mrs. Barton?" Jupiter asked.

"Just my three best friends," Mrs. Barton said. "I couldn't help it, it was so exciting to see all that treasure. How much was it?"

"Not nearly as much as you think, Mrs. Barton," Jupiter said. "And it wasn't found on Skeleton Island at all."

"Now you can't fool me, young man!" She

125

wagged a finger at him. "Tomorrow come sun-up you're going to have company out on that island. I do think quite a few people will sail over and try their luck at digging for treasure. Oh my, yes. I'd go, too, if I were a little younger and spryer. I'm sorry to say it, but local folks are a little bit peeved that you outsiders should come in and find treasure on Skeleton Island when the town is so poor and needs it so badly."

She started collecting the dishes.

"But I mustn't talk so much," she said. "Goodness, I'm just a chatterbox when I get started."

She went to the kitchen, leaving the three boys very upset.

"That does it!" Pete exclaimed. "Why, half the town will be out on Skeleton Island tomorrow. They'll never be able to finish the movie now. And I guess it's our fault."

"I guess it is, all right," Bob said. "Your father will be stopping in to see us soon, Pete. What shall we tell him?"

"We'll have to tell him the truth," Pete answered. "Won't we, Jupiter?"

"I guess we will," Jupiter agreed. "But I'm having an idea. Let me think about it for a while."

He continued thinking as Pete and Bob listlessly turned the pages of some old magazines in the parlour.

Shortly after dark Mr. Crenshaw and Harry

Norris arrived. They announced that Roger Denton would be back the following morning and shooting would begin in a day or so on the island. However, they had decided against making the short subject about the boys diving for treasure. The incident in the underwater cave was only one reason. The cloudiness of the water and Jupiter's cold also had helped them make up their minds.

Normally the boys would have been deeply disappointed, but now they had too much on their minds to give it much thought.

They told Mr. Crenshaw and Mr. Norris what had happened and the two men uttered exclamations of dismay.

"That ruins everything!" Mr. Crenshaw cried. "Why, treasure hunters will swarm all over us like locusts. We'll never convince anybody we aren't here to hunt for pirate gold."

"I have an idea," Jupiter said slowly. "I mean, it might help save the situation. Why not film all these people sailing out to the island and racing around looking for treasure? You could get a short subject out of it, called maybe, 'Treasure Fever'. You could never hire so many people, but they'll be coming of their own accord and it might make a swell picture."

Harry Norris thought for a moment.

"It's coming to me," he said. "Sure, this is a disaster, but maybe we can turn it into an asset. Say we show somebody finding some treasure, and the word gets round, and the whole town sails out to look, and we photograph them all digging . . . Yes," he turned to Pete's father, "I think we can swing it. The thing to do is to organize this treasure hunt. Now here's my idea—"

Swiftly he outlined his plan for keeping the digging under control.

"Instead of trying to keep people off the island," he said, "we'll invite them to come and dig! We'll get Doctor Wilbur to go on the local radio and invite people to dig for treasure on Skeleton Island tomorrow. We'll say we don't believe there is any treasure, but they're welcome to look. And we'll offer a prize of five hundred dollars, to be won by a draw held in the evening. That will convince them we don't believe in any treasure.

"The conditions will be that everybody who comes to dig registers with us for the prize draw, and that they don't damage the merry-go-round or the roller coaster. Then in the evening we'll be hosts for a big clambake for everyone, and hold the draw for the prize. We can shoot pictures of all the frenzied digging and we'll get an interesting short subject we can call 'Treasure Fever,' as Jupiter suggested. Then, when it's all over, people will be convinced there's no treasure and leave us alone and we can finish off the scenes for *Chase Me Faster* without being bothered."

"I think it'll work," Mr. Crenshaw said. "Let's get over to the hotel and phone Mr. Denton in Philadelphia. You boys—" he turned to The Three Investigators—"stay put. Go to bed soon. You can come out to the island tomorrow to see the fun. But for now don't get into any more trouble!"

"But Dad, about Chris——" Pete began.

"That boy can stay in jail a few days to teach him a lesson," his father replied. "Come on, Norris."

The men went out in a hurry. The boys slumped back into attitudes of despondency.

"Gosh, I was hoping we could persuade them Chris didn't do anything," Pete said. "But they won't even listen."

"Adults don't like to listen to kids when their minds are made up," Bob observed. "Anyway, Jupe, you sort of saved the day with your idea for making a short subject about the mob of treasure hunters."

Jupiter didn't answer. He was thinking again. His mind was buzzing round, going over and over the facts they had.

"Don't overdo the thinking," Pete advised him, trying to sound humorous. "You might burn out a bearing."

Jupiter coughed loudly. Then a look of satisfaction came over his round face.

"What is it, Jupe?" Bob asked alertly. "You've actually thought of something?"

129

E

"I believe I have deduced a logical reason why you found gold doubloons in that hidden cave underneath The Hand," he said.

"You have?" Pete almost shouted. "What? And use short words. This is no time for long ones."

"Bob, let's go and look at your notes," Jupiter said. "I want to read that part about Captain One-Ear and his last stand against the British again."

The three of them trooped upstairs. Swiftly Bob found the place. He read about how the old-time pirate had been surprised at night by British troops. He had fled with his chests of treasure, been chased, and landed on The H nd. In the darkness he had eluded his pursuers, but when daylight came they surrounded him and captured him.

But his treasure chests were empty, and the British realized he had emptied all the treasure overboard to keep them from getting it. And just where in the mile of water he had emptied the chests he refused to answer. All he would say was, "Davy Jones has the doubloons in his grasp and nobody will see them again until Davy Jones decides to give them up."

"Well?" Bob asked.

"Don't you see?" Jupiter replied. "If he had just dumped the doubloons overboard, he'd have said they were in Davy Jones's *locker*. But he said 'grasp.' Now what do you grasp with?"

130

"Your hand, of course!" Bob said excitedly. "Golly, Jupe, you mean——"

Jupiter nodded. "It's the only logical answer," he said. "After he saw he couldn't escape, Captain One-Ear emptied all his stolen treasure down the blowhole. Then he teased the British by saying it was in Davy Jones's grasp, meaning it was inside The Hand. Even if they had figured out what he meant, they wouldn't have been able to get it. So it stayed hidden down in that underwater cave all these years."

"Then there must be lots more!" Pete exclaimed. "Chris was right! There may still be a fortune down in that cave!"

"I don't think so," Jupiter said. "Remember, it was loose coins he poured down the blowhole. Three centuries of tides and waves have had time to bury most of them pretty deep or to carry them out into the bay. There might be a few more doubloons under the sand there, but I doubt if there are many. You found just what the ocean left."

Pete sighed. "You're always so logical. But I suppose you're right. For Chris's sake, though, I hope he finds a lot more so that he can take his father back to Greece."

The mention of Chris reminded them of his plight, and they became gloomy again. But there was nothing they could do, and soon they went to bed.

Pete and Bob fell asleep right away. Jupiter,

however, couldn't sleep. His mind was turning over with special sharpness now. There was still another mystery to be figured out. He had all the facts, he was sure, if he could only put them together correctly.

He thought about old Captain One-Ear, fooling the British by dumping his treasure down the blow-hole. Then, abruptly, a bit of conversation he had heard and almost forgotten came back to him. And all of a sudden everything clicked into place.

"That's it!" he exclaimed, sitting up suddenly. "Ten years! That's what happened. It has to be. Bob, Pete, wake up!"

The other two awoke and yawned sleepily.

"What is it, Jupe?" Pete asked. "A nightmare?"

"No!" said Jupiter excitedly. "You two have to get your clothes on and row out to Skeleton Island. I've just deduced the real secret of the island."

Rapidly he explained to them what he had just figured out. They listened with mouths open, and when he had finished, Pete said, "Jupe, you're a genius! You have to be right— it's the only answer that makes everything fit."

"I don't know why it took me so long," Jupiter said. "Anyway, I'm sure that's the answer. You get out to the island and check on my deductions. Then go down and wake up your father, Pete, and the others. Show them what you find. Then let them take over."

He looked wistful.

"I'd go with you," he said, "but I ache all over."

"You've done enough, Jupe," Bob said. "This will get us out of the doghouse, all right. It'll be nice to be a hero for a change. But why not wake up the men and have them help us hunt?"

"Because," Jupiter said, "I might be wrong. They'd be very angry at us for waking them up. If I'm wrong, you can just row back here and nobody will be the wiser."

"Well, okay," Pete said. "Though I would like to tell Dad. But we'll do it your way."

In five minutes he and Bob were dressed and had their flashlights. They tiptoed downstairs and let themselves out of the house.

Jupe lay back in bed, feeling terrible. Why did he have to catch a cold, anyway? But it couldn't be helped and there wasn't any danger—

There wasn't any danger!

A new thought hit him like a wallop from a baseball bat. Of course there was danger! There was terrible danger, if only he hadn't been so pleased with himself he'd forgotten to think about it. Why, Pete and Bob might be killed!

17

Bob and Pete in a Tight Spot

PETE PULLED HARD at the oars of the small rowing-boat, which they had been lucky to find tied up at the movie company's pier. By the dim light of the stars, they were heading for Skeleton Island.

"There it is," whispered Bob, as the island suddenly appeared like a black blob in the darkness in front of them.

Pete had a keen sense of direction. He rowed them towards the little bay near the amusement park. The land grew closer and then was on both sides of them, and Pete eased quietly forward until the bow of the rowing-boat nosed up on the sand. Bob jumped out and pulled the boat up on the beach.

"Now we have to go through the amusement park," Pete said in a low voice. "Then up the path to the cave. I wish Jupe hadn't said not to wake up Dad."

"So do I," Bob agreed. "I wouldn't mind some company now. Do you think you can find the way in the dark, Pete?"

"Sure," Pete answered. He hesitated a

moment. It was very dark, and silent, except for the little noise of water lapping up on the beach. "Well," he said, "we better get going."

He led the way, using the flashlight just long enough to get a glimpse ahead. In a moment they were inside the ghostly ruins of Pleasure Park.

The roller coaster was a big skeleton against the sky. It gave Pete a landmark, and he skirted round it and past the merry-go-round. At the rear fence of the park, he stopped.

"Darn it," he said in a low voice. "I'm going to wake up Dad. It's not because I'm nervous, although I am, but Dad ought to know what we're doing. After all, he told us to stay at Mrs. Barton's and—well, I think he ought to know what Jupe figured."

"Okay," Bob agreed, almost whispering. "Let's do that. I'll feel better, too."

They turned round. And then they stopped dead in their tracks, their hearts beating fast.

Somebody was behind them. Somebody big. Somebody who now flashed a brilliant light in their faces and growled, "All right, stand still! I've got you dead to rights!"

Both boys froze. They couldn't see a thing with the light shining in their eyes. Then a surprised voice said, "Thunderation! It's Bob and Pete! What do you think you're up to, sneaking round on the island like this?"

The man lowered the light to the ground.

135

Now the boys could see him, but they had already recognized his voice. It was Tom Farraday, the guard.

"You could have got hurt," he said. "I thought you were somebody out to damage the rides that've been fixed up. Come on now, explain yourselves."

"Jupiter figured out the secret of this island," Bob said. "We came out to see if he's right."

"The secret of the island?" Tom Farraday sounded puzzled. "What are you driving at?"

"There really is treasure hidden on it," Pete told him. "At least, Jupe is sure there is."

"Treasure?" The guard obviously didn't believe them. "What treasure?"

"Well, you see——" Pete began. But Bob interrupted.

"You helped Jupiter figure it out," he said. "You gave him the clue he needed."

"Now wait a minute!" the guard rumbled. "I don't know what you're talking about."

"The other morning," Bob said, "you were telling us how the Ballinger brothers held up your armoured truck ten years ago, stole a hundred thousand dollars, and crippled your left arm."

"Yes? What about it?"

"Well," Pete put in, "you also told us how the Ballingers were captured by the Coast Guard in a disabled boat, and how the Coast Guard saw

136

them dump some packages overboard. The stolen money, everybody thought."

"Sure it was. What else?"

"Well," Bob went on, "it was just ten years ago that someone started scaring people away from this island by starting up the story of the ghost on the merry-go-round again. Jupiter said it couldn't be a coincidence that the hold-up was ten years ago and the campaign to keep people off the island also started ten years ago. He said they had to be connected."

"I don't get what you're driving at." Tom Farraday sounded puzzled.

"Don't you see?" Pete said importantly. "The Ballinger brothers tried to make a getaway by boat and their engine broke down. They must have managed to get here to Skeleton Island and hide the stolen money. Then they pushed off again, determined that if they did get caught, everybody would think the money was lost. That way, when they got out of jail, they could come and get it and slip away quietly.

"You said yourself they got out of jail just a couple of weeks ago. But obviously they haven't come for the money yet, because with the movie company on the island they've been afraid to risk getting caught."

"Jumping fishhooks!" Tom Farraday said. "Say, you make it sound true! But supposing the Ballingers did hide the money on this island, does your friend have any idea where it could be?"

"Jupiter says it would have to be some place high and dry," Bob told him. "Canvas sacks and paper money buried in the ground would rot. The best high and dry place on the island is——"

"The old cave!" Tom Farraday exclaimed. "It has plenty of cracks in the rocks where sacks of money could be hidden."

"That's what Jupiter thinks," Pete agreed. "It's the only place high and dry enough to keep the money safely."

"Except," Bob put in, "that tomorrow hundreds of people will be swarming over this island on a mammoth treasure hunt, so someone is bound to go exploring that cave. That's why we came over right away, tonight, to look for the hidden money."

"By golly, I think you may be right!" Tom Farraday exclaimed. "Think of it, all that money hidden in that cave ten years now and nobody guessing until you kids came here. Why didn't I ever think of it myself? Well, there's only one thing to do. Let's go and see if the money really is there."

"We were going to get Mr. Crenshaw," Bob said.

"No need for that," Tom Farraday told them. "Since they have to be up so early, let them sleep. If we find the money we can lug it down and wake them up. If we don't find it, you kids can slip back home and nobody'll be the wiser."

"Well——" Pete began, but Tom Farraday had already turned.

"Follow me," he said. "I know the path."

Tom Farraday moved rapidly through the trees, the boys close behind him. The whole scene was hushed and spooky, and Bob was glad they had encountered Tom Farraday. It made him feel safer to have the big burly man along.

"Oof!" Bob grunted abruptly. Someone had stepped out from behind a tree and grabbed him. Powerful hands had him in a vice-like grip.

"Mr. Farraday, help!" Bob managed to gasp. Then a strong hand covered his mouth and he couldn't make a sound.

He heard a scuffle behind him, a grunt from Pete, and then silence. But Tom Farraday, ahead of them, was free and he had a gun. He would—

Tom Farraday turned. He didn't seem the least bit surprised. Nor did he draw his gun. "Good work!" he said. "They didn't have time to yell."

"No thanks to you!" said the man holding Bob. "Suppose they had gone to the camp first and woken up those movie people? We'd be in the soup!"

"But they didn't, Jim, and we've got them," the guard said, sounding nervous. "So it's all right."

"It's not all right," said the tall, thin man who

139

had Pete in his grasp. "Now we've got to get rid of them. But we'll tend to that later. First we get them to the boat. Then we get the money. Then we take care of these snoopy, interfering kids."

"Sure, Bill, sure," Tom Farraday agreed quickly. "Is it true what they said about the money being hidden in the cave?"

"Never mind if it's true or not. That's our business!" growled Bob's captor.

"It's my business, too!" Tom Farraday said. "After all, one third of that money is mine and I've waited ten years for it. Not to mention getting a crippled wing from your clumsiness!"

"Shut up! You talk too much!" the man called Bill said. "You'll be taken care of. Now take off your shirt and tear it into strips. We have to gag these kids and tie their hands."

"But——"

"Move!"

"All right, all right."

Tom Farraday slipped off his jacket, removed his shirt, and rapidly tore it into strips. Bob's stunned mind began to work again. Bill and Jim —those were the names of the Ballinger brothers. And now it was apparent that Tom Farraday was their accomplice! He must have helped them work out the hold-up in the first place. He had let himself be slugged to throw off suspicion, but they had hit him too hard and broken his collarbone. Ever since then he had been waiting for the Ballingers to recover the money they had hidden, so that he could get his share.

Bob's racing thoughts were interrupted as the hand covering his mouth was removed. He opened his mouth to yell, and as he did so, Tom Farraday shoved a wadded-up piece of shirt into his mouth. Another strip was tied round his head to hold the gag in place. A moment later Bob's arms were twisted behind him and Tom Farraday was tying a strong strip of cloth round his wrists. He was effectively tied and gagged.

When Pete was also bound and gagged, the two Ballinger brothers gripped them by their jacket collars.

"Now, kids," Bill Ballinger rasped in their ears, "march ahead of us. Don't try any tricks or you'll be very, very sorry! !"

Bob stumbled along over rough ground. He could hear Pete being forced along behind him. How far they stumbled through the darkness, neither Pete nor Bob could tell. But after what seemed a long time, they came out at a pebbly beach. Dimly they could see a large motor-boat drawn up on shore.

"Get aboard, you two!" growled Bill Ballinger. Awkwardly the boys climbed over the bow of the motor-boat into the open space in front of the engine.

"Now, down!" Ballinger growled and gave them a shove that sent them toppling in a heap.

"Jim, get me the fishing-line. I'm going to make sure these kids don't escape while we're busy."

A moment later Bob felt himself being wound in the heavy fishing-line, until he was tied up like a well-wrapped bundle. Then the two men rolled him to one side and proceeded to tie Pete just as securely.

As they worked, the brothers conversed in low, angry tones. They were furious at the boys for finding treasure that afternoon, and so setting the scene for a big treasure hunt. Bob gathered they had planned to wait quietly, not going near their hidden loot until it was perfectly safe. But the prospect of the island swarming with treasure seekers had forced them to take immediate action, despite the risks.

"There!" Bill Ballinger said finally. "These two little eels aren't going to give us the slip now! Come on, Jim, let's get the cash. We've lost too much time as it is."

The two men climbed out of the boat.

On shore, Jim Ballinger said in a low voice, "You stay here, Tom, and keep an eye on the boat. Give an owl hoot if you need to warn us."

"What are you going to do with them?" the boys heard the guard ask uneasily. "They'll talk, they'll implicate me——"

One of the Ballingers laughed in an ugly tone.

"They won't talk," he said. "We're taking them with us. Never mind what we plan. But after we're gone you turn their rowing-boat over and shove it out into the bay. Tomorrow it'll be found floating and folks will think they overturned and got carried out to sea."

"Well—okay. I guess that's how it has to be," the guard answered. Then there was silence as the footsteps of the two Ballingers faded away.

They heard Tom Farraday muttering to himself. "So that's why all their friends and relatives gave out phony stories about seeing the ghost! So no one would come prowling round this island! If I had only guessed I could have had all the money to myself!"

Bob lay on his side next to Pete. He tried to speak but could manage only a muffled sound. His fingers strained to reach the knots that bound his wrists, and then gave up.

18

Something Very Unexpected

THEY WERE in a real jam, Bob thought glumly. Just about the worst jam they could have got into. Jupiter had guessed correctly that the armoured car money was hidden on Skeleton Island. But he hadn't guessed that Tom Farraday was in with the men who had stolen it, and he hadn't figured that the Ballingers would be coming to get it tonight because of the big treasure hunt the next day.

Bob wouldn't let himself think of what would happen next.

He lay still and listened to the tiny ripples of water breaking against the stern of the motor-boat. Then a bigger ripple made the boat bob up and down a bit. Bob opened his eyes and saw a dark figure slipping on board over the stern.

The figure was crouched down so that Tom Farraday, on shore, could not see him. He started crawling carefully past the engine towards the two boys.

For a moment all Bob could hear was the sound of breathing. Then a low whisper reached his ears.

"Hi!" it said. "Don't be afraid. It's just me, Chris."

Chris! How in the world could Chris be here? Chris was in jail!

"I untie you," Chris whispered in his ear. "You hold very still."

Bob could feel Chris working at the fishing-line that was wound round him, then at the strips of shirt that tied his wrists and gagged him. It seemed like hours that the Greek boy struggled with Bill Ballinger's knots—but then he was free, cautiously stretching his cramped arms and legs.

"Chris——" he started to whisper.

"Shhh!" the Greek boy hushed him. "Slip back to stern, be ready to slide into water. I get Pete free."

On hands and knees Bob crawled to the stern. He wrenched off his sneakers. If they had to swim, he didn't want anything weighing him down.

A few moments later, making hardly a sound, Pete and Chris joined him.

"Over the stern!" Chris whispered. "Hold on to rudder."

There were about a million questions Bob wanted to ask, but they would have to wait. He eased himself down into the water, followed by Pete.

"Gosh!" Pete gasped in his ear. "Where did he come from?"

"I don't know, but I'm sure glad he came," Bob whispered back fervently.

Chris slid like an eel into the dark water. "Now we swim," he said. "If you swim on your side, make no splash. Follow me."

Without a ripple, he moved away, following the shoreline. Bob swam after him, wishing he had taken off his trousers and jacket as well as his sneakers.

They swam silently, their heads close to the dark water. After about ten minutes, they rounded a tiny point of land and were out of sight of the boat and Tom Farraday.

Now Chris led them ashore. They followed

him to a spot where the scrub trees came down near the water. Chris got down low and wriggled up until he could peer between two boulders. Following his lead, Pete and Bob found they could see, very dimly, the shape of the motorboat about three hundred feet away.

"Now we can talk if we keep voices low," Chris said. "They do not find us here."

"How did you get here?" both boys asked together. Chris chuckled. In whispers, he told them. Chief Nostigon had returned to the jail that afternoon pretty well convinced of Chris's innocence. He had managed to find the judge and the judge had set fifty dollars bail for Chris, which Chief Nostigon himself had put up. Then, after giving Chris a good dinner, he had turned him loose.

"I go home," Chris said. "I find my father pretty good. Neighbour lady looks after him. But I start to think. How does my knife get at scene of robbery on island? Somebody put it there, that's how, after I lose it. But where did I lose it? Then I think, I must have lost it in front of the cave yesterday when I have fun with you. Only person around to find it is Tom Farraday. I think Tom Farraday finds my knife and plants it at scene of robbery to make me look like a thief. Tom Farraday is up to something.

"I decide to watch Tom Farraday. Borrow boat from friend of my father's and row out after dark very quiet."

146

Chris had watched Tom Farraday set out on his nightly patrol of the island, and had seen him stop where the motor-boat was now beached, and flash his flashlight three times. The Ballinger brothers had paddled their boat in and come ashore. Then the noise of Pete and Bob rowing to the island had reached them.

"You do not row so good, Pete," Chris chuckled. "Make a splash. Ballinger fellows hide, Tom Farraday meets you and leads you into trap. I do not know what to do. Maybe I should go to camp, get men, but I think, suppose they do not believe me? Suppose they think I'm back to steal some more? Maybe I better stick around, see if I can help you.

"I see you put in boat and Ballingers go up to cave. I slip into the water, come and untie you. Now we watch the fun."

"You were great, Chris!" Pete said. "But what do you mean, watch the fun?"

"Shhh, Ballingers come back. Watch!" Chris whispered.

Dimly they could see the dark shapes of the Ballinger brothers join Tom Farraday. Each of them carried two big sacks across his shoulders.

"Everything all right?" Bill Ballinger asked, his voice coming clearly across the water.

"Everything's fine," Tom Farraday answered. "Listen, I want my share of the money now."

"You'll get it when we're ready," the other

man growled. "Come on, Bill dump the cash in the boat and let's get going."

They shoved past the guard and dumped their sacks into the beached motor-boat.

"The kids! They're gone!" Bill Ballinger shouted. "Tom, you cut them loose!"

"I did not!" the guard answered angrily. "They can't be gone!"

He flashed his light into the boat and saw the fishing-line that had bound Pete and Bob.

"They *are* gone!" he said, sounding bewildered. "But they couldn't be! Not right under my nose!"

"They're gone, and we're getting out of here!" Jim Ballinger growled. "Get in, Bill!"

"But what about me?" Tom Farraday objected. "For ten years I've been waiting for my share of the money. Ten years! Even if I got all of it it wouldn't pay me for the arm you crippled. And besides, if those kids are free, they'll blab and I'll go to jail!"

"That's your lookout," Jim Ballinger retorted brutally. "There's a tramp freighter waiting for us, and it's sailing for South America. Shove off, Bill."

Bill Ballinger pushed the motor-boat out into the water and hopped on board. Jim Ballinger pressed the starter button. The starter whirred but the motor did not catch. He tried again, but nothing happened.

"The motor!" Jim Ballinger exclaimed, a note

of fear in his voice. "It won't start! Tom, what did you do to the motor?"

"Not a thing," called back the guard. "But I'm glad it conked out. I only wish I could get my hands on you!"

"Keep trying, Jim!" the other Ballinger urged. "We've got to get going. We have to get out of here!"

Again and again they pressed the starter, but the motor refused to catch.

Chris chuckled with merriment.

"I pull wires off spark plugs," he said. "I fix them. They will not go any place. Now we go get men from camp and they take care of these fellows."

But before the three boys could move, they heard the sound of motors roaring towards the island. Two boats came racing towards them, searchlights stabbing through the darkness.

The Ballingers acted with panicky speed. Using oars as paddles, they moved the motorboat close to the shore. They leaped out and started running, directly towards the hidden boys.

Chris stood up.

"We stop them!" he yelled excitedly. "They do not get away!"

Chris picked up a length of driftwood and scrambled behind a big rock. As the first of the fleeing criminals came opposite him, Chris thrust out the stick and Jim Ballinger went sprawling on the beach.

Bill Ballinger tripped over him and fell, too. Chris pounced on them like a small whirlwind.

"You get me put in jail!" he shouted. "You make people think I am thief! I show you!"

He wrapped his arms round Jim Ballinger, preventing him from rising. Bill Ballinger hauled Chris off and threw him to one side. He fell against Bob and Pete, who were just coming to his aid.

But as the three boys sprawled on the ground, another element entered the fight. Tom Farraday came charging up and hurled himself at the two Ballingers. All three went down in a furiously fighting mass.

"Cheat me out of my share, will you!" the guard was shouting. "Leave me to face the music alone!"

Despite his disabled arm, Tom Farraday was as strong as a bull. The Ballingers could not get away from him. The three men rolled down the beach and into the water with a great splash. After a few moments of frenzied struggle, Tom Farraday had forced the Ballingers' heads beneath the water. They went limp.

"Let them up!" a voice roared. "You'll drown them!"

The boys had been so engrossed in the fight they had not seen the two boats run up on the beach a few feet away. Several men leaped ashore. Chief of Police Nostigon played the beam of a powerful flashlight on the three men in the water. In his other hand he held a revolver.

"Let them up, Tom, you hear me?" he shouted again.

But the guard seemed intent on drowning his two accomplices. It took four men to pull him loose from Bill and Jim Ballinger, who were hauled out of the water gasping weakly for breath.

When all three men had been handcuffed, Chief Nostigon flashed his light round and saw Chris, Pete and Bob.

"Well, you boys are all right, praises be!" Chief Nostigon said. "But Chris, how the dickens do you happen to be here?"

"He saved us and kept the Ballingers from escaping, Chief," Bob said quickly. "But golly, how did you get here? Did you guess the Ballingers would be coming after their hidden money tonight?"

"I'm afraid not," Chief Nostigon said. "I never dreamed they'd stashed away their hold-up loot on Skeleton Island. You can thank your friend Jupiter Jones. He came down to the police station about forty minutes ago with a wild tale about hidden money and the Ballingers probably going after it tonight because tomorrow would be too late.

"I don't know why I listened to him, but I did.

151

Down he went on all fours.

Rounded up some men and came out here—and by gosh, he was absolutely right!"

He turned. "Jupiter? Where are you? Here are your friends, safe and sound."

Jupiter climbed out of the motor-boat on to the shore. He came trudging towards them.

"It was stupid of me to send you out here without stopping to think that the Ballingers would be coming for the money tonight," he said. "It didn't occur to me until half an hour later. Then I went to get the chief."

"But you did think of it," Pete said loyally. "That's what counts."

"You'd have thought of it sooner if you didn't have a cold," Bob added. "Colds always slow a fellow down."

"I——" Jupe began. "I——Achoo!"

"There's enough credit for everybody," Chief Nostigon said firmly. "Between the four of you, you've solved the secret of Skeleton Island, recovered the stolen money, and got the criminals captured. That's not a bad night's work. Now you can leave the rest up to us. It's time you all got back to the mainland and into bed."

Jupiter let out another great sneeze. It sounded as if he agreed.

19

Report to Alfred Hitchcock

ALFRED HITCHCOCK looked down at the little pile of gold doubloons on his desk.

"I see you found it, after all," he said with a chuckle. "I said there was no pirate treasure left, yet you found some."

"Only forty-five doubloons," Jupiter said regretfully. "It really isn't a very big treasure."

"But treasure nonetheless, and a very interesting souvenir," Mr. Hitchcock said. "Now tell me, young Jupiter, how did you deduce that the stolen money from the Dollar Delivery hold-up was hidden on Skeleton Island?"

"Well, sir," Jupiter said, "it seemed obvious someone wanted everybody to stay away from Skeleton Island. That was why the stories of the phantom were spread around. I deduced there was something there someone was afraid might be found. The only thing of value that had been mentioned was the Dollar Delivery hold-up loot.

"The story of how the Ballingers apparently dumped it at sea was remarkably similar to the method Captain One-Ear used to fool the British. I concluded that the Ballingers had actually hidden the money and then fooled people into thinking it had been lost for ever."

"Excellent thinking!" Mr. Hitchcock said. "I suppose that after the Ballingers were sent to jail they instructed their friends and relatives to keep on spreading false stories of seeing the phantom."

"Yes, sir. Meanwhile Tom Farraday was hanging around, waiting for the Ballingers to be released. One third of the loot was his for helping set up the hold-up, and they had told him that when they got out they would pay him off. But he didn't know where it was."

"Or he might have taken it all." Mr. Hitchcock chuckled. "When the Ballingers got out of jail, they must have been very shocked to find the movie company actually camping on Skeleton Island."

"Yes, sir, they were," Jupiter said. "They didn't dare go for the money while someone was around. So they tried to drive the movie company away by thievery and sabotage at night. When Mr. Norris hired Tom Farraday, Tom just carried on the work—he did the mischief while pretending to guard the equipment."

"Including planting young Chris's knife and trying to frame him, eh?" the director said.

"Yes, sir. Also starting up the merry-go-round that first night we arrived to help spread the idea that the phantom was around."

155

"A point I would like to clear up. Exactly why were you marooned on The Hand by that fellow Sam Robinson as soon as you arrived? Not really to scare you into going home again, apparently."

"No, sir. I was wrong on that point. Bill Ballinger figured that everybody in the movie company would go hunting for us and the island would be deserted except for Tom Farraday. Then they could hurry out and get the hidden money.

"But the storm prevented them from starting for the island right away. Then Chris rescued us, and the search party returned before the Ballingers could go out and get their money. So that foiled their scheme that night."

"I see," the director murmured. "Then, of course, when it became known that hundreds of people would converge on the island to dig for treasure, the Ballingers had to take the risk of coming for it immediately. That's how Pete and Bob got caught."

"Yes, sir," Jupiter said humbly. "I should have realized that first thing. But Bob and Pete were gone before it came to me, so I hurried to the chief of police."

"That seems to clear up almost everything," Mr. Hitchcock said. "However, I have two more questions. How did the movie turn out, and what became of young Chris and his father?"

"The movie turned out fine. Mr. Crenshaw

got the roller coaster fixed up as soon as everyone learned the ghost was just a hoax. The final scene of *Chase Me Faster* was very exciting.

"Also, Mr. Denton got a good short subject from the treasure hunt. He used Chris in it instead of us, and showed Chris diving for treasure to help his father. The part with the townspeople digging on the island was very comical.

"But the best part of all is that the Dollar Delivery people paid a reward for the return of the money. Chief Nostigon and Mr. Crenshaw said that it should go to Chris, because he was the one who saved Bob's and Pete's lives and kept the Ballingers from getting away with the money. That and the money he earned from the movie was enough to have his father treated by some very good doctors, and take him back to Greece to live.

"He let us keep his share of the doubloons. Skin-divers did rush to explore the cave Bob and Pete and Chris found, but they only got a few more doubloons. Most of what Captain One-Ear poured down that blowhole had been washed away, I guess."

"Hmm," said Alfred Hitchcock. "Well, lads, you have justified my faith in you and I will be glad to introduce your account of this adventure. If any other investigation of an unusual nature comes up, you may be sure I'll get in touch with you."

"Thank you, sir."

The boys stood up. Pete gathered the doubloons on the desk and put them in a sack.

"We're saving these for our college education fund," he said. "But we all thought that since you sent us to Skeleton Island, you might like one for a souvenir."

He handed Mr. Hitchcock the best preserved of the doubloons. The director took it with a smile.

"Thank you, my boy," he said. "I'll treasure it."

As the three filed out, he tossed the doubloon in his fingers.

"Real pirate treasure," he said to himself with a smile. "Who would have thought they'd find it? I can't help wondering—what kind of mystery are those boys going to find themselves involved with next?"

Nancy Drew Mystery Stories

by CAROLYN KEENE

Don't miss the latest exciting adventures in this action-packed series!

The Triple Hoax (51)

A chance invitation to a display of magic puts Nancy on the track of a ruthless gang of con men, who will stop at nothing to satisfy their greed . . .

The Flying Saucer Mystery (52)

A camping holiday turns into a bizarre mystery for Nancy and her friends when they are threatened by an alien spacecraft. Determined to find out what is happening, Nancy sets out to investigate. But great danger lies ahead, for the UFO has sinister powers . . .

Armada

CAPTAIN ARMADA

has a whole shipload of exciting books for you

Here are just some of the best-selling titles that Armada has to offer:

- ☒ **Calculator Fun & Games** Ben Hamilton 80p
- ☒ **Oliver Twist** Charles Dickens 65p
- ☒ **4th Armada Crossword Book** Robert Newton 75p
- ☒ **Make Your Own Presents** Hal Danby 75p
- ☒ **The Secret Mountain** Enid Blyton 80p
- ☒ **The Chalet School Fête** Elinor M. Brent-Dyer 75p
- ☒ **The Hooded Hawk Mystery** Franklin W. Dixon 75p
- ☒ **The Hell Hound & Other True Mysteries** Peter Haining 75p
- ☒ **The Explorer's Handbook** Peter Eldin 75p

Armadas are available in bookshops and newsagents, but can also be ordered by post.

HOW TO ORDER
ARMADA BOOKS, Cash Sales Dept., GPO Box 29, Douglas, Isle of Man, British Isles. Please send purchase price of book plus postage, as follows:—

> 1—4 Books .... 10p per copy
> 5 Books or more ..... no further charge
> 25 Books sent post free within U.K.

Overseas Customers: 12p per copy

NAME (Block letters)
_____

ADDRESS
_____

_____

_____